"No one is to know the arrangement we've made."

When Serena nodded reluctantly, Leo went on, "It doesn't matter if I'm there or not. If you meet anyone else over the next few weeks, you're to convince them that you're happily in love with me. You're going to earn every penny of that money," he finished. "I want you playing your role every minute of the time we're out together in public."

"And in private?"

"That, Serena, is up to you."

Jessica Hart had a haphazard career before she began writing to finance a degree in history. Her experiences ranged from being a waitress, theater production assistant and outback cook to news-desk secretary, expedition P.A. and English teacher, and she has worked in countries as different as France and Indonesia, Australia and Cameroon. She now lives in the north of England, where her hobbies are limited to eating and drinking and traveling when she can, preferably to places where she'll find good food or desert or tropical rain.

Books by Jessica Hart

Wife-to-Be
Jessica Hart

Harlequin Books

TORONTO • NEW YORK • LONDON
AMSTERDAM • PARIS • SYDNEY • HAMBURG
STOCKHOLM • ATHENS • TOKYO • MILAN
MADRID • WARSAW • BUDAPEST • AUCKLAND

ISBN 0-373-03447-4

WIFE-TO-BE

First North American Publication 1997.

CHAPTER ONE

'I HATE weddings!'

Serena glowered down into her glass and wished that Leo Kerslake would go away and leave her alone. There was something unnerving about him. He was too tall, too dark, too aloof.

Too attractive.

His image shimmered amid the champagne bubbles, so clear that she might as well have been looking straight at him after all. She could picture exactly the austere, almost arrogant lines of his face, the steely set of his mouth and those eyes. . .

She had seen him first as she'd followed Candace up the aisle. He'd been standing beside a very nervous Richard, looking cool and assured and somehow over-whelming. Serena had known who he was of course. She was sick of hearing about Leo Kerslake. As far as she could make out, he was just some old schoolfriend of Richard's, but they were all carrying on as if he were some kind of superman. . . Leo was rich, Leo was successful, Leo was perfectly marvellous because he had interrupted his business trip to the States just to be Richard's best man.

Serena, who had spent the last week coping with the bride and the bride's mother's pre-wedding nerves, had not been impressed, but she had managed to bite back the tart comment that had leapt to her lips. She knew that Candace's family found her sharp tongue vaguely alarming, but for her friend's sake she had been on her very best behaviour all week. It hadn't, however, stopped Mrs Gerard eyeing her nervously, as if unsure of quite how to react to such unaccustomed restraint, nor had it stopped Serena drawing her own conclusions.

Privately, she had decided that Leo Kerslake sounded unbearable, and she'd been fully prepared to loathe him on sight, but then he had turned with Richard to watch their progress and she had found herself looking straight into his eyes.

His hair was so dark that she had automatically assumed that his eyes would be dark too, but instead they were a startlingly clear grey, so light they were almost silver. Wolf's eyes, had been Serena's first, confused reaction, and, quite unprepared for their effect, she'd stopped as suddenly as if she had walked into a wall. Before she'd had time to realise what she was doing, all the little bridesmaids and pageboys, who had been trailing along behind her and too busy waving at their mothers to look where they were going, had piled into each other at her back.

Fortunately, Candace's eyes had been on Richard and she'd been quite unaware of the confusion behind her, but there had been a few smothered smiles in the congregation and Serena had been burningly aware of Leo Kerslake's cool eyes on her as she'd disentangled pageboys from bridesmaids and rearranged them hastily in line. Pink with mortification, she had resumed her place behind Candace, and as she did so her gaze had met Leo's for a fleeting moment. His expression had been mocking and Serena had glared back at him with fierce green eyes before lifting her chin to look haughtily away.

She hadn't expected to like him, and now she knew that she didn't.

The service had seemed interminable. After that disastrous start, Serena had stared at Candace's back and tried to concentrate on what was being said, but

Leo's dark, magnetic presence on the other side of the aisle had kept tugging at the edge of her vision.

He was dark and tall and leanly built, with an aquiline nose and an air of austere power kept under rigid control. His pale grey morning suit was immaculate, the white of his collar dazzling against his tan, and as Serena's eyes had drifted, in spite of themselves, up his throat to the angle of his jaw her heart had clenched inexplicably.

Almost as if he had sensed her reaction, Leo had looked up just then, and Serena had seen the ironic amusement register in his expression as he realised that she had been staring at him. Humiliated, she had jerked her gaze away and had resolutely ignored him for the rest of the service. She had even managed to get through the signing of the register and the photographs outside the church door without once looking directly at him.

It had been more difficult to ignore him at the reception, but then, there hadn't been much need to. Leo, it seemed, was more than capable of ignoring *her*. Out of the corner of her eye, Serena had watched him moving among the guests—more often than not the pretty, female ones, she had noted sourly—with a growing feeling of pique. It wasn't that she particularly wanted to talk to him, but she *was* supposed to be chief bridesmaid. He could at least have had the decency to come over and introduce himself.

By the time Leo had finally deigned to approach her, Serena had been more than piqued; she'd been feeling thoroughly slighted, and her temper hadn't been improved by the way he'd come up quietly behind her just as she had taken a quick glance round to see that no one was watching and stuffed a whole sausage roll into her mouth.

'Do you always look this cross or is something wrong?'

Startled by the sudden voice at her shoulder, Serena choked and spluttered pastry down her front. Brushing furiously at her cleavage, she cast Leo a look compounded of embarrassment and resentment, unable to say anything at all until she had chewed enough of the roll to swallow.

The unnerving eyes were alight with amusement as he watched her desperately trying to get rid of the roll. 'You startled me,' she coughed indistinctly at last, cheeks scarlet with a mixture of effort and humiliation.

'Sorry,' he said, not sounding at all apologetic. He reached out quite calmly and picked a tiny flake of pastry lying just above the low-cut neckline of the frilly off-the-shoulder bridesmaid's dress that Candace had insisted Serena wear. 'You missed this bit,' he explained with a mocking look.

Serena took a sharp breath at the fleeting, electrifying brush of his fingers against her skin and took an instinctive step backwards. 'Do you mind?' she said frostily, furious to find that she was still burning with awareness of that one, brief touch.

'I was just tidying you up,' said Leo as if surprised at her reaction.

'I don't want to be *tidied up*, thank you!' Serena was ruffled by his cool, dark presence, which was even more overwhelming at close quarters. There was an ironic air to him that somehow left her feeling distinctly uncomfortable, and it was not a feeling that she liked at all. 'Especially not by someone I haven't even been introduced to!' she added defiantly.

'I don't think we need formal introductions, do you? I know perfectly well who you are and you presumably know who I am. After all, we're both here for the same reason—to support Candace and Richard.'

'You could have fooled me,' said Serena with a sniff, thinking of his leisurely progress around the more attractive of the wedding guests. 'I suppose chatting up all the prettiest girls is all in the line of duty?'

Too late, she heard the sharpness in her voice, and bit her lip in vexation as she realised that it held more than a hint of petulance. Leo had that sort of smug assurance that would automatically assume that she was jealous, although nothing, of course, could be further from the truth. She had been doing so well at holding her tongue, too, she thought glumly.

'At least I'm not standing around glowering, like some people I could mention.' For once the mocking voice was edged with steel. 'And you still haven't answered my question.'

'What question?' Serena held out her glass to be refilled by a passing waitress and vowed not to let him rile her.

'I wondered why you were so cross.'

'I'm not cross,' she said crossly. So much for resolution! How did other girls manage to smile and look sweet when she couldn't even manage thirty seconds? It wasn't fair.

'You certainly look it,' said Leo. 'I've been watching you all afternoon, and you don't look at all as if you've been enjoying yourself.'

Serena was astonished to hear that he had been watching her at all. 'I hate weddings!' she explained morosely. 'I can't bear all the *fuss*.'

She eyed the chattering throng without enthusiasm. The decibel level was rising as the champagne circulated and huge hats kept clashing together as women tried to greet each other by brushing cheeks.

'It's all right for you. You just jetted in last night. All you've had to do is turn up at the church this morning, but I've been here all week. I've had to listen to endless discussions about the colour of the tablecloths and how many flower displays there should be in the church, and every argument seems to have ended with either Candace or her mother in tears! Anyone would have thought the whole future of the marriage depended on whether the tablecloths were pink or green! What does it matter whether they were purple with yellow polka dots?'

She knew she was sounding fierce, but she couldn't help it. She just didn't seem to have a neutral setting like other people. Phrases like 'I don't mind' or 'I don't know' were alien to Serena. She always had an opinion, usually a strong one, and said exactly what she thought without ever considering the consequences. Friends like Candace had urged her to break the habit, claiming that she would get on so much better if she could just learn a little diplomacy, but although she did try it didn't come naturally to her.

Leo was looking unimpressed. He probably had her down as a rabid feminist, she decided. He would never guess how hard it had been for her to keep a careful guard on her tongue all week, and she made a conscious effort to sound more reasonable. 'Surely the important thing is the vows Candace and Richard make, not all this. . .' she gestured disparagingly around the marquee while she sought in vain for the right word '. . .all this palaver!'

'Very eloquent,' said Leo, with one of his ironic looks. 'I'd be more inclined to be convinced if I hadn't heard other women say much the same thing, only to give up all their fine principles as soon as there's a chance of dragging some poor, unsuspecting man up the aisle!'

'I'm not "other women",' Serena pointed out, eyeing him with dislike. Why should she bother being reasonable if he was going to be like that? 'And if you're that cynical about marriage you shouldn't have agreed to be Richard's best man!'

'I'm not cynical about this wedding,' he said. 'I've only met Candace once, but I should think she and Richard should suit each other admirably. And you're not exactly in a position to criticise, are you?' he went on. '*You* shouldn't have agreed to be bridesmaid unless you were prepared to at least try and look happy.'

Serena scowled and gestured down at her dress, a floaty, fussy affair that frilled off her bare shoulders and cascaded down to the floor. 'Would you be looking happy if you were dressed up like a dog's dinner?' she asked bitterly.

Leo studied her with his silver wolf's eyes, letting his gaze travel slowly from the wreath perched awkwardly on top of her head down to the pale blue satin shoes and back up to her face once more. It was not a face that suited frills and flounces. If it had been a little less uncompromising, she would have been beautiful. Her bone-structure was stunning and her skin flawless, but the strong, straight brows gave her a rather fierce expression which was only heightened by the stubborn tilt of her chin and the defiantly direct green eyes.

Serena felt herself colour under his scrutiny. 'Ghastly, isn't it?'

'There's nothing wrong with the dress,' said Leo coolly. 'It just doesn't happen to suit you, but that's no reason not to make an effort for Candace.'

'I have been making an effort!' protested Serena, stung. 'I've talked to all Candace's and Richard's boring aunts and I've smiled and smiled and pretended to find it amusing when people make the same old jokes about my stupid name. Don't tell *me* I haven't been making an effort!' She stuck her chin out at him belligerently. 'I promised Candace I'd be nice to everybody and I have!'

Amusement gleamed in the cool grey eyes regarding her, banishing that uncomfortable cynical look. 'You haven't been very nice to me yet.'

'I haven't had an opportunity to be nice to you!' snapped Serena, still peeved that it had taken him so long to work his way round to her. 'Or was I expected to join the queue?'

Leo didn't answer her directly. Instead he considered her thoughtfully. 'I'm beginning to see what Richard meant when he said you were an "interesting character",' he said after a moment, and Serena was unable to decide whether he sounded disapproving or amused.

'People always say that when they're too mealy-mouthed to say they don't like you!'

'I don't suppose anyone ever accuses you of being mealy-mouthed,' he said in a dry voice.

'I just say what I think,' said Serena with a fierce green look. That was precisely the trouble, Candace was always pointing out. People found such disastrous frankness intimidating, she would explain, but whenever Serena tried being anything less than entirely truthful she always felt a complete fraud. She couldn't win, she had decided, and always ended up being herself again. If Leo Kerslake didn't like it, that was too bad! 'And if you were about to say how inappropriate my name is please don't bother!'

'The thought never crossed my mind.' Leo held up his hands in mock-surrender. 'I imagine having a name like Serena Sweeting is rather a trial,' he went on as she subsided.

'Especially when you're neither sweet nor serene,' said Serena glumly.

He looked at her, at the proud tilt of her head and the defiant green eyes beneath the straight dark brows. 'I must admit that you're not exactly what I was expecting,' he commented after a moment.

'Don't tell me! You thought I'd be petite and pretty and skip around tossing my curls over my shoulder and trilling with laughter?'

'And cuddling a puppy,' Leo agreed, deadpan, but his eyes gleamed appreciatively and, in spite of her best efforts to glower, Serena was forced to laugh. It certainly wasn't a trill, but a much deeper, richer, more infectious sound that softened the uncompromising lines of her face and warmed her green eyes.

'Exactly! No wonder you were disappointed!'

Something stirred in Leo's gaze. 'Who said I was disappointed?' he asked very softly, and Serena stopped laughing abruptly as her eyes met his and her heart did a neat somersault, landing back in place with a painful thud. Afraid that she was going to drop it, she put her glass down unsteadily on the edge of a table.

She wanted to say something clever, something flippant to prove that she wasn't in any danger of taking him seriously, but her breath seemed somehow stuck in her throat, and it was only with an enormous effort that she managed to drag her eyes away from his.

'You're wrong about Richard not liking you, anyway,' said Leo in a conversational tone, quite as if he hadn't noticed that sudden tense silence. 'He does, although I suspect he finds you rather intimidating. He thinks you don't approve of him marrying Candace.'

Candace's engagement had been one occasion when Serena *had* been able to keep her mouth shut. She might be uncompromisingly straightforward, impatient, even tactless at times, but she was never unkind and, knowing that Candace would be hurt by any criticism of Richard, she had kept her own reservations to herself. It wasn't her fault she was cursed with a transparently readable face. She wished she had Leo's ability to look inscrutably aloof. Life would be much easier!

She had done her best to disguise her doubts about the engagement, but she just wasn't any good at hiding her feelings, and Candace had soon seen through her. Fortunately, they had been friends a long time, and Candace had merely laughed and assured Serena that she would change her mind once she got to know Richard better.

Serena still wasn't entirely convinced. 'I just think they're rushing into things,' she said to Leo, wishing she had some pockets to stick her hands in. They felt empty and awkward, and she was reduced to picking up her glass again. Why couldn't bridesmaids wear jeans? 'Richard asked Candace to marry him after two days, and they've only known each other the time it takes to organise the wedding. It's not very long to decide if you really want to spend the rest of your life with someone or not, is it?'

'Don't tell me you don't believe in love at first sight either?' The cynicism was back in Leo's voice.

Serena glanced at him and for some reason found herself remembering how her heart had jolted when he had turned and looked at her for the first time. Faint colour stained her cheekbones and she looked away. 'No,' she said. There was a tiny pause, then, 'No,' she said again more firmly, unsure of whether she was trying to convince herself or Leo.

'You're obviously the cautious type,' he mocked.

Serena thought of her mother's worn face, of the way she had put up with years of hectoring criticism from her father. She thought of Madeleine, crying on the phone the night her husband left her. Then she thought of Alex—Alex with his blue eyes and his careless grin and his careless lies.

'I've learnt to be,' she said with a trace of bitterness.

Leo took a sip of his own champagne, studying her over the rim of his glass with those light, unsettling eyes. 'Love's a risky business, isn't it?' he agreed. 'Candace and Richard have obviously decided to take a chance on it. Sometimes you have to.'

'You haven't.' Serena looked back at him challengingly.

'I haven't taken a chance on marriage,' he amended. 'And I've yet to find a woman prepared to take a risk on me rather than on my money.'

'You're very cynical.'

'I've learnt to be,' he quoted her words back at her with a twisted smile, and as Serena's eyes met his almost unwillingly she felt her heart give an odd lurch.

'It looks as if today was the nearest either of us is going to get to the altar, doesn't it?' she said, oddly breathless.

'It was certainly quite close enough for me,' Leo agreed with certain grimness about his mouth. 'I don't intend to lose my freedom to anyone.'

'Freedom'. It seemed an odd word for him to choose. By all accounts he was a successful businessman of some kind. Serena would have expected him to talk about independence, or lack of commitment, but freedom suggested something more. It suggested space, wide skies, empty horizons; what would a businessman know of those? And why the suspicion about women and their motivations?

Serena studied him under her lashes, reluctantly intrigued. He hadn't looked that suspicious when he was chatting up every pretty girl in the marquee!

The suddenly awkward silence was broken by a passing waitress who offered them a tray of canapés. Leo took one, but Serena shook her head, with a brief smile of thanks.

'Richard tells me you and Candace are in business together,' Leo said eventually.

He was obviously only making conversation, but

Serena's face closed. 'We *were*.' Whenever she thought about all the hard work she had put into making the business such a success her heart twisted. 'We built up a really successful catering business together. It took about five years, but we'd established our reputation, and were just starting to do demonstrations and lessons as well as the usual parties and receptions. And then Candace met Richard one day and that was that.'

'What happened?'

'Candace wanted to sell her half of the business so that she and Richard could put down a deposit on their new house, and I couldn't afford to buy her out.' If she hadn't had to send that money to Madeleine, she might just have been able to scrape enough together. . .but what was the point of ifs? It was too late now.

'Couldn't you have found another partner to buy Candace's share?' Leo asked, frowning slightly.

She shook her head. 'We tried that, but in the end it was easier to sell the business as a whole, equipment, goodwill, everything.' Her voice was flat and she twisted the stem of her glass round and round between her fingers.

'So what are you going to do now?'

'I'd really like to open my own restaurant, but I can't afford to at the moment. If only I had some money. . .'

Serena spoke almost to herself, but Leo's expression hardened. 'It always comes down to money, doesn't it?' he sneered. 'I suppose that's the real reason you don't like this marriage. It's nothing to do with Candace and Richard not knowing each other, and everything to do with the fact that you've lost out financially!'

'That's not true!' flared Serena, green eyes flashing dangerously. 'It may interest you to know that I'm very fond of Candace. I wouldn't be here dressed up like the fairy on top of the Christmas tree if I weren't.'

'If you were as fond of her as you claim to be, you

wouldn't even be thinking of money at the moment—although I sometimes wonder if women ever think of anything else!'

'Sometimes we don't have much choice,' Serena retorted angrily, thinking of Madeleine and the ghastly mess she had been left to deal with. 'We don't all inherit vast fortunes,' she added nastily. 'Some of us have to go out and earn a living, which is why I'm starting a new job on Monday. I swore I'd never go back to doing directors' lunches, cooking for a bunch of fat, overfed businessmen who can't tell the difference between pâté de foie gras and a tin of dog food, but I will because it's the only way I'm ever going to make enough money to get myself back on the ladder.'

'Haven't you tried finding yourself a wealthy man to support you?' asked Leo with the same cynical edge to his voice. 'That's what most women would do. So much easier than working!'

'I've told you before, I'm not most women,' said Serena coldly, her eyes very clear and green. I don't trust men, and I won't rely on one to support me. The only person I rely on is myself. As you pointed out, I'm the cautious type.'

Leo raised one dark eyebrow. 'Cautious or scared?'

'Sensible,' she corrected him firmly, lifting her chin, and quite suddenly he smiled. The effect was devastating. His teeth flashed white against his tanned skin and one cheek creased as amusement dented the corners of his mouth. For the first time she noticed the laughter-lines starring beneath his eyes and it was as if the floor had suddenly opened beneath her, sending her plummeting into a dark, dangerous attraction.

'You don't look the sensible type to me,' he remarked.

'How *do* I look?' she asked haughtily, and was quite unprepared for his answer.

'I think passionate would be a better word,' he said, a speculative look in his eye as he studied her. 'Yes, definitely passionate!'

'What do you think of Leo?'

Serena looked across the dance-floor to where Leo was dancing with an attractive blonde. He was smiling down into the girl's upturned face as they moved languidly together in time to the music, and as he swung her round his hand slid slowly down her spine. Serena felt something clench inside her and jerked her eyes away.

'If you must know, I think he's arrogant, conceited and downright patronising!'

'Really?' Candace looked at her friend in astonishment. 'I think he's charming, and you must admit that it was a very funny speech, especially considering the poor man must be suffering from jet-lag.'

'It was all right,' Serena allowed grudgingly, remembering how the laughter had gusted around the marquee. She had smiled politely as Leo had replied on her behalf to the bridegroom's speech, but her eyes had been hostile. He hadn't wasted any of that obvious charm and wit on *her*.

'I didn't think he was going to be here tonight, anyway,' she went on. 'Wasn't he supposed to be so busy and important that he had to fly back to New York immediately after the reception?'

'That was the original plan, but apparently he told Richard he'd changed his flight so that he could stay for the dance after all.'

'No prizes for guessing why, either!' said Serena with another sour look at the blonde, now clinging to him with an adoring smile. Did they call that dancing? Any closer and they'd have to prise them apart!

'He's very attractive, isn't he?' said Candace, following her look.

Serena deliberately turned her back on Leo, but his image flickered tantalisingly in her mind: the lean, powerful body, the cool, dark, angular face and the ironic gleam in those unsettling eyes. She could picture exactly the angle of his jaw and the way the lines around his eyes had deepened when he smiled.

'If you like that overbearing type,' she replied with studied casualness.

Unfortunately Candace had known her a long time. 'Aha! So you *do* think he's attractive!' she cried triumphantly.

'All right, he's very good-looking,' Serena admitted with something of a snap. 'It doesn't mean I have to like him.'

When he'd been talking to her she had felt like a cat with its fur brushed up the wrong way, all too conscious of the cool mockery in his eyes. 'Passionate', he had called her. She felt as if the word was still vibrating through her, in spite of the fact that it was nonsense and he had obviously been joking. He hadn't even bothered to disguise the fact that he found her faintly ridiculous, she remembered resentfully.

She dragged her attention back to her friend.

'That's a pity,' Candace was saying. 'We were sure you'd like him. In fact——' she leant forward confidentially '—Richard and I were rather hoping that you and Leo might get together.'

'What?' Serena's expression was appalled. 'You're not serious!'

'Why not?' demanded Candace, all reasonableness. 'You'd be perfect for each other. Richard says that since he came into his inheritance Leo's always been surrounded by women, but what he really needs is someone strong enough to stand up to him, and you need a man like Leo who won't be intimidated by you.'

'I don't need *anyone*,' Serena corrected her with emphasis, aware of an odd feeling at the pit of her stomach at the very idea of being with Leo.

'Yes, you do,' said her friend placidly. 'All men aren't like Alex, you know. You can't let one experience put you off men for life.'

'It isn't just one experience,' she protested. 'My sister thought she needed a man, too, and look where it's got her! She gave up her training to go to Florida with Chris and now she's stuck there struggling to bring up three children on her own. The one time she *does* need a husband, he runs off with his secretary!'

She could have mentioned her father too, but he had died before she had known Candace, and she had kept her memories of his harsh presence to herself.

'Madeleine was unlucky,' Candace was saying. 'It doesn't have to be like that. Look at me and Richard. I know you think we're rushing things, but it just feels right to be together. That's how it could be for you, Serena, if only you could find the right man. You've always been the one to support your family—first your mother, now Madeleine. You need someone to lean on—to look after *you* for a change. Someone who can get through that prickly exterior of yours and find out how warm and funny and kind you really are underneath.'

'Leo Kerslake doesn't strike me as a man who's particularly interested in *kindness*,' said Serena a little waspishly. She had turned unthinkingly back to the dance-floor, but Leo and his clinging blonde had disappeared, no doubt to seek some dark corner together. 'And even if he was I'm certainly not interested in *him*! You'll have to find someone else to practise your matchmaking skills on, Candace. Leo Kerslake is the last man I'm likely to fall in love with!'

'Why's that?' asked a cool, mocking voice at her shoulder, and Candace and Serena swung round, both aghast to find Leo standing behind them, a look of unmistakable amusement on his face. Shock had made the glass jerk in Serena's hand, slopping wine down her dress, and she brushed at it futilely.

'Do you make a habit of creeping up behind people?' she demanded, instantly on the attack. 'That's the second time you've done that to me today!'

'I'd hardly say that I was creeping,' said Leo, quite unperturbed. 'It's not my fault that you were both so engrossed in your conversation that you didn't see me.'

'Not being blessed with eyes in the back of my head, I wasn't likely to see you anyway,' said Serena crossly. 'And you shouldn't have been eavesdropping!'

'All I heard was you insisting very loudly that you would never fall in love with me.' Leo smiled reassuringly at Candace, who was looking guilty, then looked back at Serena, still rubbing at the wine stain on her dress. Her head was bent, and he could see the hair which earlier had been tied up and smothered with ribbons and a floral wreath.

Serena's hair was her glory, her one vanity. Long and thick and shining, it was a beautiful deep coppery colour, much brighter than brown but nothing like red. Tonight she had swept it up and away from her face, securing it in a heavy knot at the nape of her neck with a dramatically carved African wooden comb.

'I have to confess that I didn't recognise you at first,' he said. 'It was only when I heard you loudly voicing your opinions that I realised it was you after all!'

Serena lifted her head at that and found his eyes travelling appreciatively over her flame-red dress. In complete contrast to the bridesmaid's dress she had been wearing earlier, it was very plain, but the simple design emphasised the willowy slenderness of her body while the brilliant colour was a good foil for her striking features.

There was a strange expression in Leo's eyes as he completed his scrutiny, and, hardly aware of what she was doing, Serena straightened slowly. 'You look. . . quite different,' he finished, after an odd, tense pause.

She wished she felt different. Instead, she felt just the same as she had when she had talked to him before—edgy and unsettled and unsure of herself.

'All I've done is change my dress,' she snapped. 'Is that so remarkable?'

She could see Candace wincing at her tone, but Leo seemed amused more than anything. She hated the way he privately seemed to find her ridiculous. Why couldn't she be cool, like other girls? Why couldn't she smile and answer lightly, instead of biting his head off and making a complete fool of herself?

Not that Leo seemed bothered. 'The change is remarkable,' he answered smoothly.

Candace looked from one to the other with sudden interest. Serena was standing clutching her glass, rigid with hostility, a vibrant figure in her red dress and with her vivid, defiant face. She was a tall girl, but Leo looked down on her easily, as dark and cool as she was fiery. His expression was unreadable.

'Why don't you two go and dance?' Candace suggested brightly. 'There are still masses of people I didn't get to talk to at the reception, so I'd better carry on circulating.' Ignoring entirely Serena's look of anguished protest, she whisked herself away.

The hotel ballroom was seething, but Serena felt as if she and Leo were standing alone, isolated in a bubble of tension. Risking a glance at him, she found herself looking straight into his eyes. They were cool and light in his dark face, and for some reason she felt the breath dry in her throat while something warm and scary uncurled deep inside her.

'Well?' said Leo after a moment. 'Shall we take Candace up on her suggestion?'

Serena's cheeks burned at the ironic note in his voice and she jerked her eyes away. Why was she standing there staring at him like an idiot?

'You'd better ask someone else,' she said belligerently, taking a gulp of wine to hide her confusion. She knew she was being rude and ungracious, but rudeness was the only defence she had against. . .what? She wasn't even sure what it was that she needed to guard against; she only knew that Leo made her feel edgy and uneasy, as if he threatened everything she stood for just by being there. 'I can't dance.'

Wordlessly, he removed the glass from her hand and set it down on a nearby table. 'Then we'll just have to hold each other, won't we?' he said, taking her hand in a firm grasp and leading her on to the floor before she had time to protest further.

Other couples were dancing up and down with abandon in time to the music, but instead of releasing her Leo put his other hand in the small of her back and pulled her against him. Instinctively, Serena tried to pull away, but his grip only tightened and in the end she was forced to give in and rest her free hand gingerly on his shoulder, holding herself stiffly as far away from him as she could.

'Relax,' he ordered with that same hateful mockery in his voice.

'I can't,' she muttered. 'I've told you, I can't dance.'

'I'm not asking you to perform at the ballroom championships,' he pointed out, acidity edging his tone. 'All you've got to do is stand here and sway in time to the music. That's not so difficult, is it?'

Serena bit her lip. The difficulty wasn't swaying, it was ignoring the magnetic tug of his body. She could feel the strength of his shoulder beneath her hand. What was it Candace had said? Something about her needing someone to lean on. It would be very easy to lean on Leo. He was just the right height for her. She could lean against his hard, reassuringly solid body and rest her face against his throat and let his arms encircle her and hold her close. . . She was terrified at how vividly she could imagine how comforting it would be.

Comforting, but very, very dangerous. She had never needed anyone to lean on before, so there was no reason to start now. There was no reason for the thought of relaxing against him to be so suddenly, irresistibly appealing.

Fixing her eyes on a spot just below his ear, Serena tried to ignore the feel of his fingers wrapped around hers, the pressure of his hand against her spine. Remember Alex, she told herself frantically; remember how you vowed never to trust another man again; but, even as she held herself rigidly away from Leo, the prospect of leaning closer mesmerised her. She could almost feel the rock-like security of his body, the warmth of his skin below her lips. . .

So vivid was the image that Serena stumbled and Leo had to tighten his arm about her to stop her falling. 'For heaven's sake!' he said irascibly. 'Stop trying to lead me round the floor! I know you're keen to prove how independent you are, but I'm sure your feet would do less damage if you just relaxed and let me do all the work.'

With that, he pulled her unceremoniously against him, and held her so tightly that she had no choice but to sway in time with his body.

CHAPTER TWO

SERENA couldn't breathe. Her heart was pounding, drowning out the sound of the band. Could Leo hear it? Could he feel the heat strumming just beneath her skin? Her head was so close to his. She closed her eyes so that she wouldn't see it, but she was acutely aware of his closeness all the same. Another inch and her temple would brush his cheek, a little more and her face would fit so comfortably into the angle of his jaw. . .

'You still haven't told me why you're not likely to fall in love with me,' said Leo conversationally into her ear, and, recalled abruptly to reality, Serena jerked her head away from his as if from a blow.

'Why should I fall in love with you?' she demanded, shaken back to reality.

'No reason. I just wondered why you felt the need to be so adamant about it, that's all.'

Serena looked over his shoulder. 'I think you should know that Candace is planning to try her hand at matchmaking. Now that she's married, she thinks that everybody else ought to be married too. She and Richard have apparently decided that we would suit each other perfectly!'

'Do I gather from the acid note in your voice that you don't agree?' asked Leo, swinging her expertly round to avoid bumping into another couple.

'Of course I don't! Quite apart from the fact that you're just not the sort of man I find attractive, I'm obviously not your type either.'

'Oh? What makes you say that?'

'Observation,' said Serena curtly. 'Judging by the girls you've been dancing with this evening, I'd say you have a decided preference for simpering blondes!'

Leo's silver eyes glinted appreciatively. 'I'm flattered to think that you've been watching me so closely, but you're quite wrong, you know. I can't think of anyone I've danced with this evening who lives up to that description. You certainly don't and I'm dancing with you, aren't I?'

'Under duress,' she reminded him. 'You wouldn't have asked me if Candace hadn't made it almost impossible for you not to.'

'Wrong again, Serena. I wanted to see whether you lived up to the promise of that dress.'

She glanced up at him sharply. 'What on earth do you mean?'

'You wear it like a challenge.' said Leo. 'As if you're daring a man to discover whether you're as fiery as you look. Is that why you wear it, Serena? To put off the cowardly types?'

If anything, the opposite was true. Serena wondered what he would say if she told him that it was the brave men she wanted to put off. For he was right, in a way. Her fierceness was a shield, a thorny hedge to keep out intruders. She didn't want anyone to know how vulnerable she was behind it. She had let down her defences for Alex, and Alex had hurt her. She wasn't going to hurt like that again. She wasn't going to end up like her mother, or Madeleine.

She wasn't going to tell Leo the truth, either. 'No,' she said coolly. 'I wear it because it's the only evening dress I've got.'

He laughed suddenly. 'It looks as if Candace has got her work cut out making a match for you, Serena! Perhaps she should have thrown that bouquet to someone a little more willing.'

'Yes, she should!' said Serena vengefully, remembering the embarrassing scene. One minute she had been standing near the car waiting to say goodbye, as Candace and Richard left the reception in a flurry of confetti, and the next something had come hurtling through the air towards her. She had caught it automatically before realising that it was Candace's bouquet and, looking up in consternation, had found herself looking right into Leo Kerslake's ironic grey eyes. 'I don't know why she bothers. She knows I don't ever want to get married.'

'She obviously doesn't believe that you mean it if she's set on matchmaking.'

'Well, I do mean it!' snapped Serena.

'Is it marriage that scares you, or just getting involved?'

'Nothing *scares* me,' she said defiantly.

'Then why do you put up all your prickles as soon as a man comes near you?'

'Just because I haven't fallen into *your* arms, it doesn't mean I'm like that with everybody!'

That wasn't quite true, either. Most men retreated in alarm after the first few minutes, but Leo wasn't alarmed and he wasn't intimidated and she didn't know how to deal with him at all.

'Doesn't it? Every man I've seen you dancing with tonight has looked thoroughly intimidated,' he said, almost as if he could read her mind. 'I've got a theory about girls like you,' he went on, ignoring Serena's outraged look. 'I think you're cowards beneath all that bluff. I think you're afraid of love and passion and desire because, deep down, you don't think you'll be able to control it.'

'I've never heard such rubbish!' returned Serena, furious at being lumped in the category of 'girls like you', and more than a little rattled by his perception, which was a bit too close for comfort. 'I'm not afraid of anything!'

'Brave words, but are you sure about that?'

'Of course I am!'

Leo looked down into her indignant face and then shook his head. 'I'm not convinced,' he said. 'I think that red dress is all bluff. Underneath that fiery exterior lies a girl who'd run a mile at the first sign of anyone taking her up on its promise.'

'No, I wouldn't,' she protested, too angry to realise that he was deliberately provoking her.

An odd light gleamed suddenly in his eyes.

'Can you prove that?'

Too late, Serena looked wary. 'What do you mean, prove it?'

'Show me that you're not scared of me.'

'Scared? Of you?' She managed a scornful laugh. 'You must be joking!'

'Well?' Leo taunted her. 'Are you prepared to prove what you say?'

'Certainly,' she said, lifting her chin in a characteristically proud gesture.

'Then kiss me,' he said.

Serena tripped over Leo's feet, making him wince. The band had launched into a particularly loud and boisterous number, and the floor seemed to reverberate with the beat.

'Sorry,' she muttered, thinking that she must have misheard. Leo couldn't possibly have challenged her to kiss him. 'What did you say?'

'I said, kiss me,' he repeated calmly.

Serena's stomach turned over and disappeared, leaving her with a strangely hollow feeling inside. 'Don't be ridiculous,' she said weakly. 'I can't do that.'

'Why not?'

'I'd have thought it was obvious,' she said, recovering slightly. 'I hardly know you.'

'You know enough about me to decide that you're never going to fall in love with me,' he pointed out with unanswerable logic.

Serena changed tack. 'I can't go around kissing strange men. It's too dangerous.'

'You're surrounded by two hundred people,' said Leo, casting an eye around the crowded ballroom. 'What could be safer than that?'

'If you think I'm to make an exhibition of myself in front of all these people, you've got another think coming!'

'All right, on the terrace.' His gaze mocked her. 'Or are you too scared after all?'

'You're a fine one to talk.' With the nasty feeling that she was being backed into a corner, Serena, typically, went on the attack. 'You were the one who said you wouldn't risk marriage. That makes you scared too!'

Leo swung her round once more. How was he managing to dance and carry on this bizarre conversation? she wondered wildly. 'We're not talking about marriage, Serena. Like you, I'm too sensible to commit myself to marriage, but it doesn't mean I'm afraid of my own feelings.'

'Nor am I!'

'You can't expect me to believe that if you won't prove it,' shrugged Leo.

'All right!' she snapped, incapable of backing down from a direct challenge. 'I'll prove it.'

'Go ahead,' he said, releasing her, and she looked up at him uncertainly.

'Now?'

Around them, one or two dancers had begun to cast curious looks at the way they were facing each other without moving—a still, tense centre to the gyrating dance-floor. Candace danced past and raised her eyebrows questioningly. 'On the terrace,' Serena said to Leo, changing her mind abruptly.

Outside, the night air was soft and cool against her flushed skin. 'I can't believe I'm doing this,' she said helplessly, watching Leo prop himself against the stone balustrade and spread his arms in invitation. The moonlight threw his face into relief, highlighting his cheek and nose, just catching the line of his mouth, the gleam of his eyes.

'Well?' he prompted.

Serena swallowed. She would have to go through with it now, she realised fatalistically, wondering how she could possibly have allowed herself to be manoeuvred into such a ridiculous situation.

Taking a deep breath, she walked towards him, rested her hands lightly on his shoulders and planted a brief kiss on the corner of his mouth before stepping hastily back out of arm's reach. She felt very odd, as if her insides had tangled themselves into a great knot, making it hard to breathe. Her lips were throbbing where they had brushed so fleetingly against the tantalising coolness of his, against the warm, male-rough texture of his skin.

She cleared her throat. 'There. Happy now?'

Leo shook his head slowly. 'Coward,' he said.

'What do you mean?' demanded Serena, firing up indignantly. 'You dared me to kiss you and I did!'

'Do you call that a kiss?' Leo raised his brows provocatively. 'I thought for a moment that you were going to be brave enough to kiss me properly, but obviously I was wrong.'

Serena's eyes flashed. She wasn't going to let him get the better of her now that she had got this far! 'All right,' she said furiously. 'Let's see if this will convince you!'

Stepping up between his knees, she took his face impatiently between her hands, too angry to feel nervous now. Leo made no attempt to hold her. His arms were relaxed by his side, his hands resting on the balustrade as Serena looked into his eyes, her face bright with challenge in the moonlight. A smile glimmered in the silver depths looking steadily back at her, and for a moment her nerve faltered before she dropped her gaze resolutely to his mouth.

And suddenly it was easy. It was almost as if she had been thinking about this since he had turned in the church and their eyes had met for the first time. It was almost as if she had already kissed him a thousand times before, as if her lips had been made to fit with his. It was as if she had forgotten that she was only doing this to prove a point and was kissing him because she wanted to know how his mouth would taste, how cool and firm his lips would be, how his skin would feel beneath her hands.

Very slowly, she leant into him until her mouth touched his, gently at first and then, as her courage grew, more persuasively. She felt his lips curve into a half-smile, and then he was kissing her back, lifting one hand to pull her against him while the other tugged at the comb in her hair. It dropped unnoticed to the terrace as the thick, shining coil untwisted and tumbled down her back, and he tangled his fingers in it to gather her closer.

Serena was lost. At the first touch of their lips the kiss had leapt beyond control, and her mouth moved instinctively against Leo's in sweet discovery as sensation upon sensation shivered along her senses. She had forgotten that she hardly knew him, that she didn't like him, that he had deliberately provoked her. All that mattered was the feel and the touch and the taste of him, and the dangerous, explosive excitement pounding through her.

Her fingers drifted down his cheeks to his jaw before, with a murmur of pleasure, she slid her arms around his neck and sank deeper into his kiss, letting Leo take control, letting him press her closer to the hard heat of his body, letting his mouth explore her warmth.

'I'm convinced,' he murmured against her ear a long, long while later.

'Convinced?' echoed Serena hazily, obscurely resentful that he had broken the kiss at last. She let her lips drift over his jaw, lost in a whirl of sensations and quite unable to think beyond the taste of his kiss and the feel of the steely muscles beneath her hands.

'I take it all back,' said Leo, running a lock of silky hair through his fingers. 'I think you've proved beyond doubt that you're not scared of me or yourself.'

Reality hit Serena like a dash of cold water. With an audible gasp, she jerked out of his arms as the full enormity of what she had been doing hit her. 'You. . . you. . .' she stammered incoherently, unable to string a sentence together through the jumble of surging emotions.

'I what?' asked Leo politely.

Serena was horribly conscious of her tangled hair and ragged breathing, and her face burned at the realisation that Leo was utterly unmoved by the whole encounter. He just sat there with that cool expression of his while her heart pounded and her knees shook uncontrollably. It was sheer pride that kept her upright and tilted her chin.

'I hope you're satisfied now,' she managed at last, appalled to hear how husky her voice sounded.

'Oh, I am, I am,' said Leo. 'I infinitely prefer your passion to your prickles, Serena.'

'That wasn't passion,' she said unsteadily, moving away from him so that he wouldn't see the lie in her eyes. She folded her arms protectively around her to stop her hands shaking. 'That was just a kiss to shut you up.'

'In that case, I'm impressed.' He got easily to his feet and crossed to where she stood, poised for flight. He put one finger under her chin and lifted it so that she had to look up at him, her eyes huge and defiant in the reflected light from the ballroom. His voice was soft, but the mocking undercurrent still ran through it unmistakably. 'If that's how you kiss when you're making a point, Serena, how do you kiss when you're in love?'

His body was tantalisingly close. Serena wondered if he knew what an effort it was for her to jerk her chin out of his grasp and step away from him. 'That,' she said, marvelling at how steady her voice sounded now, 'is not something you're ever likely to find out.' And, turning on her heel, she stalked back into the ballroom with her head held high.

Serena banged the van door shut and grimaced as she stooped to pick up the carrier bags. Only her third week at Erskine Brookes and already things were going wrong!

It was all Leo Kerslake's fault, she thought vengefully as she marched across the car park towards the service entrance. Time and time again she had replayed the scene on the terrace in her mind, thinking of what she should have said or should have done. She should have been coolly dignified and laughed off the whole idea, refusing to let herself be provoked like that. What she *shouldn't* have done was put her arms around his neck and kiss him as if she loved him.

The memory of his dark, ironic face, of the touch of his lips and the feel of his hands in her hair had haunted

Serena for the last two weeks. She hadn't seen or heard
from Leo since she had walked away from him on the
night of Candace's wedding, but she still burned whenever she thought about him, which was far too often for
her own peace of mind. She presumed that he had gone
back to the States, and was quite certain that he had
never given her or that scene on the terrace another
thought. It irked Serena that she couldn't do the same.

At odd times of the day she would find herself
remembering how he had looked when he had smiled
and how it had felt to be held in his arms, and she
would screw her face up furiously whenever she realised
what she was doing. She had never wasted so much
time thinking about a man before—not since Alex,
anyway—and she wasn't about to start now.

In an effort to put him from her mind Serena had
thrown herself into her new job, but cooking lunch for
a few directors every day was far too easy for a cook of
her talents. Erskine Brookes was a privately owned
merchant bank and, while the directors did a lot of
entertaining in the dining-room, their tastes were con-
servative to say the least.

She wished now she'd found a job that was more of a
challenge—at least it would mean she wouldn't have so
much time to think about Leo Kerslake—but the money
at Erskine Brookes was excellent and she really
couldn't afford to give it up yet. If she ever wanted to
save enough to open her own restaurant, she would
have to stick with the boring, well-paid jobs, and, more
immediately, there was Madeleine to consider.

Serena frowned as she thought of her sister. Poor
Madeleine had been left with a whole lot of financial
problems as well as three small boys when her husband
had run off, and when he and his new wife had been
killed in a car accident all her problems had been
compounded.

In spite of being the elder, Madeleine had always tended to rely on Serena for support when things went wrong. It had been Serena who had looked after their mother's affairs, and Serena who had flown to Florida to help Madeleine over the first dark days after her husband left. Now, if she could only pay off the worst of Madeleine's debts and see her settled in some sort of job, she could start saving for her own future.

Madeleine had rung at the weekend as usual. She was still looking for a job, but it was difficult with three boys to look after at the same time. Serena had suggested that she move back to England but Madeleine had been adamant that she wanted to bring the boys up in America. 'Their father was American, and they're American,' she had said. 'And, frankly, I feel more American than English now. No, I'm going to stay here. This is where the boys belong, and England's got too many bad memories for me.'

Serena had known that she was thinking of their father. He hadn't been a big man, and Serena couldn't remember him ever raising a hand to any of them; his cruelty had been more subtle than that. His weapons had been a savage tongue, a tyrannical disposition and standards so impossibly high that they could never be met.

He had wanted a son, and their mother had borne the brunt of his disappointment at having only two daughters instead. From being a bright, pretty girl, she had been worn down by years of humiliation and criticism into a timid, faded creature. Serena felt angry whenever she thought of the way her mother's life had been wasted. Deprived of kindness and respect, she had come to think of herself as being worthless in the end, and, by the time her husband had died, it had been too late to restore her self-esteem.

Madeleine, too, had quailed beneath their father's

temper. Like her mother she had felt inadequate and marriage to an American had offered her the chance of escape. Serena had always been stronger, and had learnt to stand up for herself in a way that filled Madeleine with awe. Like all bullies, he had picked on the weakest, and he had known that his youngest daughter wasn't cowed by his constant carping and criticising. When he had died Serena had been conscious only of relief, and then resignation, when she had realised that she was going to have to carry on being strong for her mother and her sister who had never learnt to look after themselves.

Looking back, she wasn't surprised that Madeleine's marriage had failed. Her father had made sure she had no confidence in herself, and her husband hadn't been much better. It was left to Serena to support and encourage her as much as she could. If Madeleine could only get herself a job, Serena was sure her confidence would grow. When she had suggested sending some money, so that the boys would be able to go to summer camp during the holidays, Madeleine had demurred at first, but allowed herself to be persuaded in the end with Serena's assurance that it would be much easier to look for a job without distractions. Madeleine had changed the subject away from her own problems then, wanting to know about the wedding.

'Did you meet anyone nice?' she had asked hopefully. It never failed to amaze Serena that Madeleine's disastrous marriage hadn't made her any less interested in romance.

Leo's image had shimmered in front of Serena. 'No,' she'd said firmly, and had changed the subject just as quickly back again, but the damage was done. It had been impossible to get him out of her mind after that. She had tried everything. She had scrubbed the kitchen floor and gone for brisk walks around the common, but still the memory of his kiss had simmered at the edge of her mind.

Eventually, in desperation, she had rung a friend and allowed herself to be talked into going out to a night-club in the hope that that at least would succeed in putting Leo out of her mind. It had worked too but, as she hadn't got to bed until three that morning, she had ended up oversleeping.

She had leapt out of bed with a yell when she'd woken up and seen the time. Punctuality had been stressed when she'd first joined Erskine Brookes. The personnel officer who had interviewed her had confided that the chairman came down like a ton of bricks on anyone spotted coming in late, and, while Serena couldn't care less what the chairman thought, she had her own professional pride; unless she raced, she would never get lunch ready in time.

After that, of course, everything had gone wrong. The journey from her small flat in south-west London to Erskine Brookes in the City was bad enough at the best of times, but that morning one of the bridges was blocked and Serena had spent forty minutes trapped in one spot, drumming her fingers furiously on the van's steering-wheel.

She had planned to buy some fresh ingredients on her way, but a frustrating search for fresh dill had done nothing to improve her temper. In the end she had had to change her menu completely and buy a whole new set of ingredients and, by the time she eventually got to Erskine Brookes, she was ready to bite the head off the first person who dared to speak to her.

From the front, the bank was an imposing building. Huge wooden doors let into a vast entrance hall, the air hushed and redolent of generations of accumulated money. Waiting for her interview, Serena had eyed the oil-paintings and the deep red leather sofas and wondered how such an old-fashioned institution managed to survive in today's cut-throat financial world, but since then she had seen the array of modern technology in the offices upstairs, and now knew that the fuddy-duddy impression Erskine Brookes gave at first was deceptive.

Not that she had much to do with the bank. Serena was single-minded when it came to work. As far as she was concerned she was there to cook, and she had little interest in what went on outside her kitchen. It didn't matter to her that she was restricted to using the service area at the back of the building. There were no oil-paintings or comfortable sofas back here, but it was functional in the extreme, and that was all Serena cared about.

Kicking her way through the service doors, she was mentally revising her work plan so that she could get lunch ready in time when she saw a note propped against the lift doors. 'Out of Order'.

'Great!' she muttered, putting down the bags and massaging her sore fingers where the plastic had been cutting into them. 'That's all I need!'

She glanced at the stairs and then down at her bags. Damn it, why should she toil up nine flights when there were perfectly good lifts in the entrance hall? It had been explained to her in painstaking detail that, as cook, she was not to use the visitors' lifts under any circumstances, but Serena was not about to be put off by a stupid little regulation like that.

Picking up her carrier bags once more, she stalked through to the main entrance hall and across the marbled floor to the elegantly discreet lifts, ignoring the receptionist's look of horror, and jabbed the call button.

Fortunately, she was so late that there were few people about and, in spite of her bravado, Serena was secretly relieved when the doors slid open to reveal an empty lift. Heaving the contaminating carrier bags out of the receptionist's offended sight, she leant back against the wall with a sigh and waited for the doors to close. They were halfway across when a man stepped smartly through the gap and turned to look at her as the doors sighed firmly together.

It was Leo Kerslake.

'Hello, Serena,' he said.

It might, of course, have been the motion of the lift, but Serena felt as if the floor had dropped from beneath her. The colour drained from her face and for a moment she felt completely numb before an astonishing surge of emotions brought the colour rushing back to her cheeks. Shock, incredulity and irritation mixed with a hastily suppressed burst of joy at the sight of him chased each other across her transparent expression, and for a few seconds she could do nothing but stare at him, opening and closing her mouth ridiculously like a landed fish.

It was unmistakably Leo. She had spent the last two weeks trying to forget every line of his face, every angle of his body, and now that he was here he was suddenly *more* than she remembered. His eyes were lighter, more penetrating, his hair darker. He seemed taller, more powerful, more overwhelming. Only his mouth was exactly as she remembered it, a cool, firm line that knotted her stomach.

'I thought you were in the States.' It was the first thing that came into her head.

'I came back at the weekend.'

He didn't seem the slightest bit surprised to see her, she realised. If anything, he sounded resigned, with an edge of irritability, and she was suddenly conscious of the fact that her cheeks were still flushed with temper from the morning's frustrations and that her hair was tumbling messily over her shoulders. She had been in so much of a hurry when she scrambled out of bed that she hadn't had time to tie her hair back neatly as she usually did.

In fact, she probably looked just as she had done on the terrace, and the thought sent a fresh surge of colour up her throat. If they *had* to meet again, it might at least have been when she was looking cool and efficient and professional. As it was, she could read the derision in his eyes and knew that she just looked a mess.

He, of course, was looking immaculate in a dark suit and a pale blue shirt. His tie was a darker blue with a gold crest. Serena was convinced he had dressed simply to put her at a disadvantage.

'Are you here on business?' she demanded sharply.

He lifted an eyebrow at her tone, 'Yes.' He glanced down at the carrier bags around her feet. 'What are *you* doing here?'

'Working,' she said shortly.

'Do you always use these lifts when you're laden with shopping?'

Serena bristled. 'What's it got to do with you?'

'It doesn't create a very good impression,' said Leo, looking down his nose. 'Visitors to the bank shouldn't have to fight their way through a sea of plastic bags to get to a meeting.'

'Perhaps the bank's other visitors aren't as snooty as you,' said Serena crossly. 'No doubt you'd prefer not to have to mix with *hoi polloi*, but the service lift isn't working, and I don't see why I should have to labour up nine flights of stairs just to spare you the indignity of sharing a lift with a few carrier bags! Although if I'd known I was going to have to share a lift with *you*,' she went on after a moment's reflection, 'I think I would have taken the stairs after all!'

Leo shook his head. 'I see you're as charming as

ever! You should really be a little more careful about who you talk to like that, Serena.'

She knew she should, but she had had a frustrating morning and there was something about Leo Kerslake that got under her skin. 'You may impress Candace and Richard with how rich you are, but it doesn't make you God's gift to the financial world,' she snapped. 'We don't all share your opinion of how important you are!'

'It's nothing to do with importance,' said Leo, and the steeliness in his voice made Serena quail inwardly. 'It's a question of courtesy. Do the directors here let you talk to everyone like that?'

'How the directors run Erskine Brookes is none of your business,' said Serena bravely, but noted with relief that the lift had stopped and the doors were sliding open to reveal the foreign exchange floor. She had wondered for a nasty moment if he was coming all the way to the ninth floor with her!

Leo stepped out. Turning, he leant his hand against the metal doors to stop them closing again. 'You should learn to control that temper of yours, Serena,' he told her in a deceptively mild voice. 'One of these days it'll get you into real trouble,' he added as he stood back and the doors closed between them.

Serena stared at the polished steel, suddenly aware that her knees were trembling. Her wretched tongue! She had been in the wrong, of course. As an employee of Erskine Brookes, she should never have spoken to a visitor like that, but how could she have helped it when Leo had stood there in that infuriatingly cool way and given no sign at all that the last time they had met, he had held her between his hard hands and kissed her until she had forgotten everything but the rocketing excitement of his touch?

Guilt souring her temper even more, she dragged her shopping along to the kitchen and began putting it away with much muttering and slamming of cupboard doors. Why did Leo have to pick this morning and this bank and that lift to go visiting? It was all his fault. If he hadn't been so provoking at the wedding she would never have kissed him, and she wouldn't have had to waste so much of her time trying to forget him.

He was the only reason she had been out last night— normally she hated nightclubs!—which made it his fault that she had overslept this morning. If he told whoever he was visiting how she had spoken to him she would lose her job, and *that* would be his fault too! He had probably caused that traffic jam this morning as well, *and* bought up every bunch of dill in London.

She was rolling out pastry when Lindy, the chairman's secretary, put her head round the door. 'Have you got five minutes?' Lindy was rather nervous of Serena, unsure of whether to admire or be alarmed by her forthrightness. 'The chairman would like to meet you.'

Serena looked up and wiped her forehead with the back of her arm. 'Can't he wait until this afternoon?' she asked irritably. She had talked herself out of feeling guilty about Leo into an even more belligerent mood than usual. 'I'm busy.'

Lindy was evidently shocked at the very idea of suggesting that the chairman should wait. 'He said he'd like to see you now.'

'He'd probably also like lunch served promptly at one o'clock,' snapped Serena, giving the pastry an aggressive turn. It wasn't fair to take her bad temper out on Lindy, she realised with a twinge of guilt. The pastry had borne the brunt of her mood and would probably be ruined as it was! 'I can't be expected to have everything ready if I have to run around kowtowing to chairmen all morning! What does he want to see me for, anyway?'

'He likes to meet everyone who joins the bank,' Lindy explained nervously. It doesn't matter if it's a new director or a new junior for the photocopying-room. He would have seen you before, but he's been away. He's only just got back.'

'Well, if he's waited two weeks to meet me, he can wait a few more hours, can't he?'

Lindy looked as if she would like to wring her hands. It was obvious that she couldn't decide whether she would rather face Serena's wrath or the chairman's. 'He did say just five minutes,' she offered placatingly.

Serena gave an exasperated sigh. If she refused to go it would only get poor Lindy into trouble, and it wasn't Lindy's fault some puffed-up chairman expected everyone to jump as soon as he snapped his fingers. 'Oh, very well,' she said irritably, folding up the pastry with deft hands and pressing down the edges with a rolling-pin. 'This will have to rest anyway.' She covered the pastry and put it in the fridge, brushing the flour briskly off her hands. 'Let's go and get it over with.'

'Er. . .you've still got your apron on,' Lindy pointed out as she trailed along in Serena's fiery wake. 'Wouldn't you like to take it off before you see him?'

'No, I wouldn't,' said Serena. 'He knows I'm a cook, doesn't he? I don't suppose he'll be expecting a fashion parade.'

'Well, no. . .but he is the *chairman*,' said Lindy in reverent tones.

'So?' Serena was in no mood to be impressed. 'That doesn't make him a god, and even if it did I don't see why I should tart myself up for him.'

Lindy looked after her helplessly. Like almost every-one else at Erskine Brookes, she didn't know quite what to make of Serena. Most of the directors were just as much in awe of the new cook as the most junior secretaries, although those of the staff who had actually had to deal with her had thawed when they'd discovered that while her tongue might be sharp it was never cruel, and that her intimidating image covered an unexpected kindness and charm.

The chairman was a more formidable proposition, though. Lindy wondered if she should try and warn Serena, then decided that she might as well save her breath. Serena was probably more than capable of looking after herself.

The chairman's office was on the floor below the kitchen and dining-room. Serena stalked down the stairs, glad that there was no reason to use the lift and run any risk of bumping in to Leo Kerslake again. She hoped he'd finished his business and gone. The last thing she wanted was to bump into *him* again.

Lindy, seeing that Serena was likely to march straight into the chairman's room without even bothering to knock, nipped prudently ahead of her and opened the door. 'Serena Sweeting to see you, Mr Kerslake.'

Sheer momentum was carrying Serena into the room even as she heard what Lindy had said, but she stopped dead on the threshold. 'What?' she said stupidly, feeling a yawning hole opening up beneath her. 'What did you say his name was?'

'You heard right the first time,' said Leo, getting up from behind his desk, his silver eyes gleaming with mockery. 'Thank you, Lindy,' he added to his secretary who cast Serena a curious glance before withdrawing reluctantly and closing the door behind her.

'You're not the chairman,' said Serena blankly, as if to convince herself that this was all just a horrible dream.

'Funny—that's what my board of directors would like to think too,' Leo told her with a distinct edge to his voice. 'Unfortunately for you and for them, I *am* the chairman of Erskine Brookes.'

CHAPTER THREE

'BUT . . .' Serena was still standing stupidly by the door. 'Why didn't you tell me?'

He shrugged. 'It isn't a secret. If you'd bothered to look, you'd have found my name on the bank's notepaper. Frankly, I'd have expected you to have made it your business to find out who the chairman was. It's only professional to know exactly who you're dealing with.'

'I'm professional where it matters—in the kitchen,' Serena asserted, stung, but Leo was patently unimpressed.

'You'll forgive me if I say you don't look very professional at the moment,' he said, eyeing her up and down so that Serena was acutely conscious of her floury apron and the piece of kitchen string which was all she had been able to find to tie back her hair. She had a nasty suspicion that there was a smudge of flour on her cheek as well, but she didn't want to draw Leo's attention to it by rubbing at it.

Leo pointed at a chair. 'You'd better come and sit down.' He had taken off his jacket and loosened his tie and the sleeves of his shirt were rolled up to reveal muscled forearms, but the casualness did nothing to disguise the sense of power and authority he exuded. Serena would have liked to resist his peremptory order, but somehow she found her feet taking her across the room and sitting her down exactly where he pointed. Annoyed by her own subservience, she sat straight-backed and glared mutinously up at him.

'I should also point out that you don't behave very

professionally either,' said Leo, propping himself against the front of his desk and folding his arms. It reminded Serena all too vividly of the way he had propped himself against the balustrade on the terrace, and memory throbbed insistently deep inside her. She couldn't take her eyes off his hands. On the terrace, they had pressed against her spine, slid through her hair, held her against him. . .

Hastily, she jerked her attention back to what he was saying. 'If I'd met you for the first time in that lift today, I have to say that I wouldn't have been impressed.' His tone was astringent. 'Erskine Brookes doesn't expect its employees to turn up to work in jeans and a T-shirt with their hair all over the place, nor does it allow them to clutter up the main lift with plastic carrier bags.'

'Does Erskine Brookes allow its employees to breathe without its permission?' Serena retorted, fighting back the only way she knew how. She knew that he was right, but she just didn't have it in her to bow her head and listen meekly to his strictures. Besides, it wasn't entirely her fault.

'If you'll remember, I was in that lift because *your* other lift had broken down and hadn't been repaired, and those carrier bags you're making such a fuss about were full of ingredients to feed *your* directors. I wasn't carrying them around for the fun of it.

'And as for my clothes, I don't see that it matters what I wear in the kitchen as long as it's clean and practical. Or do you expect me to cook in a pin-striped suit just in case the Chancellor of the Exchequer decides to drop in and sample a few of my rock cakes?'

'I expect you to behave in a courteous and professional manner at all times in the bank,' said Leo with a blistering look. 'If I thought you spoke to anyone else the way you spoke to me this morning, you'd be out of here before you had time to pick up your rolling-pin.

'Fortunately for you, there are two factors in your favour: one, that you are, apparently, a superlative cook, and two, I understand from the staff I've spoken to that you can be really quite charming when you try. I've heard all about the special cake you made for the cleaning lady's birthday, and the way you helped Bob Chambers' secretary when she had to stay late by making her a pudding for her dinner party.'

'I did that in my own time,' Serena said defensively. 'It didn't cost the bank anything apart from a little electricity.'

'Oh, I believe you,' said Leo. 'I just think it's a pity you keep your undoubted charm so well hidden most of the time. You like to give the impression of being tough, but you're not nearly as hard as you like to pretend. After all,' he went on, his eyes on her mouth, 'I have better reason than most to know just how soft and warm you can be when you try.'

The colour flooded into Serena's cheeks and she jumped to her feet without thinking, as the memory of that wretched kiss flickered and burned between them. She could taste his lips again, feel his tongue twining around hers, feel his hands hard against her body.

Unable to look at him in case he should see the memory naked in her eyes, Serena stalked to the window and wrapped her arms around her. 'Did you know at the wedding that I would be working for you?' she asked stiffly.

'No. If you remember, you were very unforthcoming. You were determined not to be interested in what I did, or you might have discovered the coincidence before I did. I only found out when I came back this weekend and had time to catch up on some paperwork.

I recognised your name on a report I was sent on changes in personnel since I'd been away.'

'I didn't realise you were a merchant banker,' Serena told him a little sulkily. 'Richard just told me you'd inherited a lot of money.'

'I did—all my mother's shares in this bank. She was the last of the Erskines, so I've inherited all the family shares. That makes me—against all expectation, I know—the chairman of Erskine Brookes. This makes me very unpopular with my board of directors and my cook, but I don't feel like giving up my position to make either you or them happy! It also means that if you want to be paid for working here you're going to have to learn to do things my way. Now, come and sit down again. I want to discuss how you're going to work.'

Serena set her jaw stubbornly. 'I decide how I'm going to work,' she stated, but she found herself doing as he said.

'No, Serena,' said Leo, his face implacable as he resumed his place behind his desk. 'This is my bank and you work for me. If you want this job, you're going to have to accept that I'm the one who makes the decisions round here. In spite of what you think, I can assure you that I'm more than capable of telling the difference between pâté de foie gras and a can of dog food, so I want to see your planned menus every week.'

'Haven't you got more important things to do?' asked Serena crossly. 'What's the point of employing me to plan menus if you're going to fiddle around with them anyway? You might as well do it yourself!'

'I don't expect to have to change anything,' Leo told her coolly. 'But I like to know what's going on every-where in Erskine Brookes, from the kitchen to the boardroom. That means I'll know if you're talking to anyone else the way you talk to me! I expect you to employ that charm you undoubtedly possess beneath all those prickles, preferably at all times but particularly when you come across anyone visiting the bank, in the lifts or elsewhere.'

'I'm paid to cook, not stand around making small talk,' said Serena defiantly. 'If you don't like my cooking you only have to say so and you can find yourself someone else.'

Leo sighed. 'You really must learn not to be so hasty, Serena. Are you really prepared to give up a well-paid job out of pique?'

Serena longed to be able to tell him what he could do with his job, but then she remembered Madeleine. She had promised to send the money for the boys to go to summer camp, hadn't she? And well-paid jobs weren't that easy to come by.

She gritted her teeth. 'No,' she conceded. 'But only because I need the money. I didn't realise that sucking up to the chairman would be part of my duties!'

'I suppose you want a bonus for being nice?'

'That would be handy,' she said, deliberately ignoring his sarcasm and looking him straight in the eye. 'How much are you offering?' She regretted the words as soon as they were out.

'That, Serena, would depend on how nice you were prepared to be,' said Leo, and she felt herself grow suddenly hot.

When would she learn to think before she spoke? Her eyes slid away from his and she got abruptly to her feet once more. 'If there's nothing else, I'd better get back to the kitchen.'

'Of course,' he agreed smoothly, and rose as well. 'Oh, you might want this back,' he added as an after-thought, pulling open one of his desk drawers and tossing the carved wooden comb she had worn on the night of Candace's wedding across the desk towards her. 'At least it would be an improvement on that piece of string!'

Serena picked up the comb as if it were hot. 'Where did you get this from?' she asked, but even as the words came out of her mouth she knew the answer.

'You left it on the terrace. It fell from your hair while you were—er—otherwise occupied.'

'You mean when you were kissing me?' she said, facing him with challenging eyes, uncomfortable awareness submerged in a familiar wave of anger. The memory was so vivid between them, they might as well bring it out into the open.

Leo quirked an eyebrow at her. 'As I remember it, you were kissing *me*.'

'Only because you provoked me!'

'And very nice it was, too.' Leo smiled as he walked across and casually wiped the smudge of flour from her cheek with his thumb. 'Now *that* would be worth a bonus!'

Serena was horrified by the electric reaction of her body to the careless brush of his fingers. Her face quivered and tingled where he had touched her cheek, and she jerked back from the mesmerising effect of his nearness.

'I may be desperate for money, but I'm not that desperate!' she said, thoroughly unnerved by her own response. 'You can keep your precious job if it means being that nice to you!' she added defiantly, and marched out of the room, slamming the door behind her.

Lindy's expression of incredulity as Serena had come storming out of Leo's room had changed swiftly to sympathy. It was obvious that people who crossed Leo Kerslake didn't last long in Erskine Brookes and, when Serena had calmed down a bit, she had lived in hourly expectation of receiving a notice from Leo telling her that her services were no longer required.

But no notice had come that afternoon, or the next day, and gradually Serena relaxed. It seemed that Leo hadn't taken her seriously after all. Well, there was no surprise in that, but she couldn't help feeling a little piqued that he hadn't bothered to come and talk her out of her decision to leave. He had obviously assumed that she would think better of it, and it went against the grain to prove him right, so much so that she was almost tempted to resign after all, just to show him! Only a serious recalculation of her finances persuaded her that she would be mad to throw in such a well-paid job and, in the end, she gritted her teeth and carried on cooking.

She saw little of Leo over the next two weeks. Occasionally, she would catch a glimpse of him in the dining-room as she carried in a new course, but he was always absorbed in a business discussion and didn't even acknowledge her presence. Serena knew that she ought to be pleased, but peeved would have been a more accurate way to describe her feelings. She might as well have been a piece of furniture for all the notice he took of her!

Sometimes she saw him walking down a corridor or disappearing round a corner just as the service lift opened, and every time her heart would lurch uncomfortably. Serena hated the way it did that.

Leaving the office one Tuesday evening, she was waiting in her van to turn out of the car park when she saw Leo walk out of the front entrance with his hand under the elbow of a lovely girl. She was smiling up at him, her hair golden in the summer evening sunshine. In her beautifully cut pale pink suit and elegant shoes, an indefinable but unmistakable aura of wealth and glamour hung around her.

Abruptly aware of her own faded jeans and worn T-shirt, Serena's fingers tightened on the steering-wheel as she watched them cross the road. Leo's dark head was bent down to his companion's, and they laughed intimately together.

Serena couldn't help wondering if Leo had told the girl his views on freedom. He didn't much look like a man determined to keep his life free of entanglements right now! Had he meant what he had said, or did he just warn women off automatically while he waited for a girl who would be worth giving up his freedom for? Would that girl be blonde and beautiful and smiling in the sunshine? For some reason, Serena felt a little sick at the thought.

Only the aggrieved blast of a car horn behind her recalled her attention. Hastily putting the van into gear, she drove off in the opposite direction, reminding herself that she couldn't care in the least what Leo did in his spare time or whom he did it with.

She could remind herself till she was blue in the face, but still the image of Leo's hand under the girl's elbow stayed imprinted on her mind. She tried everything to blank it out, without success, and, by the time Candace phoned later that evening she was thoroughly glad of the distraction.

'Come round to supper tomorrow night,' Candace invited after Serena had asked about their honeymoon in the Maldives. 'Then we can have a real chat. You can see the wedding photos, too.'

Serena wasn't all that sure she wanted to spend an evening looking at photos that would only remind her of Leo—she was reminded of him quite enough as it was!—but it would be better than spending another evening alone trying not to think about him, and it would be nice to see Candace again.

'I'd love to,' she said.

* * *

The next day she was even more glad that she had arranged to go out when she came across Leo and his blonde girlfriend again—this time in the dining-room. Serena almost dropped the tureen of soup she was carrying when she saw them sitting together at the head of the long table. The rest of the board of directors were there too, but it was obvious that the girl had eyes only for Leo.

Since there had been no request for a formal lunch, Serena put the soup on a hot plate on the sideboard and let them help themselves. She had made fresh rolls, too, wrapped in a linen napkin to keep them warm, and the tantalising smell drifted through the dining-room. Even Leo looked up when she brought them in, and their eyes met with a jarring impact as she leant over to put the basket on the table. The basket tipped from her suddenly nervous hands and the hot rolls tumbled all over the table, effectively bringing the entire conversation about the strength of the pound to a halt.

'Sorry,' she mumbled, but in her haste to pick up the rolls she knocked over a glass of water. 'Sorry, sorry. . .'

Scarlet with embarrassment, she mopped up the mess and retrieved the rest of the rolls, conscious all the time of Leo's light eyes on her. He didn't say anything, but she caught his glance just before she finally escaped from the room, and knew from the mocking look that he was well aware of what had caused her confusion.

Furious with herself, Serena took care not to look anywhere near him when she cleared the soup away and brought in the next course, but she was very aware of his magnetic presence at the end of the table. It was a relief when the meal was over; it was a relief when the *day* was over. Everything that could go wrong had gone wrong, and Serena took a taxi to Candace's and Richard's new house feeling in need of a strong drink.

Candace was looking tanned and pretty and positively glowing with happiness as she hugged Serena. 'I can't tell you how wonderful married life is!'

She ushered her into the sitting-room, only to bump into her as Serena balked in the doorway. Leo was standing by the mantelpiece talking to Richard, but he broke off as he caught sight of her.

'I didn't know you were going to be here!' she said without thinking.

'You're just as much a delightful surprise to me too,' said Leo coolly. His silver-grey eyes held an odd expression, a mixture of amusement, exasperation at her determined antagonism and something that might have been appreciation of the picture she made in the doorway, her face vivid with hostility. She was wearing the inevitable jeans but with an emerald-green shirt, and her beautiful copper hair fell loose for once around her shoulders.

'We thought it would be cosy to have just the two of you,' Richard put in hastily. 'Bridesmaid and best man, you know. Besides, you'll want to see the video of the wedding.'

Serena could think of few things she would less rather do. 'We were there, Richard,' she pointed out. 'We know what it was like. Couldn't we see the photographs of the Maldives instead?' Her suggestion held more than a tinge of desperation.

'You can see those afterwards,' said Candace, who was used to Serena. She handed her a glass of wine. 'The video's such fun. Put it on now, darling,' she added to Richard.

Leo and Serena were placed firmly together in front of the television while Richard ceremoniously loaded the video and switched it on with a flourish. 'You'll love this,' he said to Serena, who doubted it. Forgetting her dislike, she stole a glance at Leo and caught his eye.

The look they exchanged was pregnant with resignation, and Serena suddenly felt much better. It was suprisingly comforting to know that he was as bored by all this as she was.

The video rolled interminably through the ceremony and the reception. There was Candace looking bridal, Richard looking sheepish. There was Leo, poised and imperturbable, and Serena, in that hideous dress, looking cross and gloriously out of place. She felt Leo's eyes flicker towards her once or twice, but stared resolutely ahead.

Then they moved on to the dance in the evening. Was it never going to end? Serena stifled a yawn and then stiffened as she saw herself on the screen, vibrant in her red dress. She was dancing with Leo, or rather swaying with him. They drew the eye amid all the other couples bopping up and down around them, as if they were alone in their own private world.

Serena saw Leo's hand sliding down her back, and her spine tingled now as it had done then. She saw herself, eyes closed, leaning against him, and she remembered how mesmerisingly comforting his body had been. Leo's head was bent slightly, his face half hidden from the camera by her hair, and it was impossible to see his expression.

Serena didn't dare look at him now. Instead, she shot a glance at Candace, who opened her eyes innocently and gave her a bland smile.

'You two look as if you were enjoying that dance,' said Richard, with the laugh that was already grating along Serena's nerves. 'No one would guess you'd met each other for the first time that day. Anyone would think you were in love!'

'Don't be ridiculous, Richard,' said Serena sharply, conscious of a hollow feeling inside. 'We were dancing, that's all.'

'If you can call that dancing. . .' Richard winked suggestively at Leo, who merely gave a cool smile that gave absolutely nothing away.

'We were merely trying to avoid treading on each other's toes.'

Richard laughed again and nudged Candace. 'That's your story!'

Serena sat simmering on the sofa, unsure of whether to hit Richard or Leo or simply stalk out of the room. Of all the moments, the camera *would* have had to capture that one! How could she have looked so relaxed and at home in Leo's arms, as if she belonged there? She hadn't felt in the least bit relaxed! She could still remember how her pulse had boomed in her ears and every nerve had tingled at his nearness.

She ought to think herself lucky the camera hadn't followed them out on to the terrace, she thought with grim humour. *That* would have made quite a shot! Was Leo too remembering what had happened after that dance?

Sliding him a sidelong glance under her lashes, she found his silvery pale eyes resting on her with an unreadable expression but, as he noticed her look, he sent her a conspiratorial smile.

The video blared in the background, rolling on to its conclusion, but Serena hardly noticed. She felt oddly weightless, held by Leo's smile, imprisoned by memories of his lips and his hands and the hard security of his body. Her throat felt tight and there was an insistent strumming deep inside her.

And Leo knew. He knew exactly what she was thinking about. Serena saw his smile twist as an ironic gleam sprang back into his eyes and with an enormous effort she jerked her gaze away, the colour flooding up her throat.

Mercifully, the video had come to an end, but there

was an awkward pause as Richard got up to remove the cassette. Leo was looking typically self-contained, unperturbed by the silence, while Serena sat rigidly at the end of the sofa, as far away from him as possible, her face betrayingly flushed, looking as if she would happily murder anyone who commented on it.

Candace cleared her throat, deciding it was time to change the subject. 'Tell us about your new job, Serena. Are you working for anyone nice?'

Serena risked another glance at Leo, furious to find that his eyes were alight with amusement at her expense. 'I don't think "nice" is quite the word I'd use to describe him,' she said tartly.

'Serena is working for me,' Leo explained when Candace looked baffled.

'Really?' Candace sat up straighter, obviously intrigued. 'What an amazing coincidence!'

'Amazing,' Serena agreed with something of a snap.

Richard looked at Leo with jovial sympathy. 'I bet she's not the easiest of employees! How on earth do you handle her?'

Leo glanced at Serena, who glared back at him with fierce green eyes. 'With care,' he said.

For Serena, the evening seemed endless. Once the video was over, they had to admire the photographs and the presents and the new house. Serena loved Candace dearly, and she was glad that her friend seemed so happy, but all the newly-wed coyness soon grated on her nerves and it was a real effort to keep her tongue between her teeth.

When Leo explained that he had an early start at the bank the next day and offered her a lift home, she was so grateful that she quite forgot how much she disliked him.

'Thank you,' she said with a gusty sigh of relief as she

settled into his car. It was long and low and luxurious and smelt of leather and wealth. She clicked on her seatbelt and settled back comfortably. 'The only thing I can say about this evening is that it's reminded me why I never, ever want to get married!'

'You certainly didn't look as if you were enjoying yourself very much,' said Leo, switching on the engine, which sprang into life with a low, throaty purr.

'The wedding was bad enough without having to sit through the video as well,' complained Serena. 'I'm surprised they weren't handing out T-shirts! And why has Candace taken to beginning every sentence with "Richard says" or "Richard thinks"? She used to be able to think for herself before they were married!'

'But that's not the real reason you're so anti-marriage, is it?' said Leo, glancing at her before looking in the mirror and pulling out into the road.

Serena went still. 'What do you mean?'

'I was talking to Candace before you arrived. She told me about Alex.' He paused. 'She said he broke your heart.'

'I thought he did at the time, but, looking back, I think he just taught me a good lesson.' She looked straight ahead, watching the lights shimmering on the wet road. 'Did she tell you he was married?'

'Yes. She also told me that you were very young.'

'I was twenty-one, and too stupid to realise the real reason he was so vague about some things. Then his wife found out and came to see me.'

The memory still had the power to make her hands shake and she clasped them together in her lap.

'It was awful,' she went on in a low voice. 'She was completely destroyed by Alex's deception, and he'd let her think that I was the one manipulating him—demanding that he leave her and marry me. I vowed then that I'd never let a man put me in the position she was in, grovelling to another woman to ask for your own husband back!'

For a moment she was silent, remembering Alex's wife who had reminded her so bitterly of her mother. Her father had never cheated on her, but he had humiliated her just as much in other ways. She wished she had remembered that before she'd got involved with Alex. She wouldn't forget again.

They were slowing down to stop at a pedestrian crossing and Serena straightened, recalled to the present and the man sitting so cool and detached beside her. Leo didn't want to hear about her youthful follies. 'Candace had no business discussing me with you!' she asserted with a strong sense of grievance.

'She cares about you,' said Leo unexpectedly. He waited for a car to pass, then turned out on to the Fulham Road. 'She told me that you'd helped her over lots of problems in the past, and that you'd never once said anything to her about having to sell the business, although she knows how much it meant to you.'

'Oh, well. . .' Serena shrugged, embarrassed by how much Candace must have told him. 'I suppose it'll all work out for the best. At least it's given me the incentive to start saving for my own restaurant. That's what I really want.'

'Is it?' Leo cast her a long, speculative look as they waited at a red light. 'Are you sure you don't have a secret hankering to be married like Candace after all?'

Serena tried to imagine herself in Candace's position, married to a man like Richard. Richard was nice enough, but he would drive her up the wall. If she was to share her life at all, it would have to be with someone with a stronger will than hers—not tyrannical like her father but someone who would respect her independence, someone who wouldn't quail when she lost her temper or look blank when she made a joke. Someone a bit like. . .

Serena's eyes drifted to Leo's strong hands on the steering-wheel, to his mouth lit by the dull, reflected light from the dashboard and her heart plummeted into abrupt, instinctive denial of her thoughts.

'Quite sure,' she said, far more firmly than was necessary.

'In that case, I may be able to help you.'

'Help me?' She stared at him, thrown by the apparent change of subject. 'I don't need any help.'

They were driving over Albert Bridge. Below them the reflected lights gleamed on the still, dark surface of the Thames. 'I've got a proposition to put to you,' said Leo.

'What sort of proposition?' she asked, instantly suspicious, and he threw her a sardonic glance.

'A financial one.'

'A job?'

'In a way. . .look, how much further is it to your flat?'

'It's the next turning,' said Serena in surprise, pointing.

'In that case, can I explain it to you when we get there? It's rather complicated.'

'All right,' she agreed, baffled.

Typically, whereas she always had to leave the van at the other end of the road, Leo managed to find a parking-space right outside her flat. Serena was very conscious of him behind her as she tried to unlock the door and her fingers fumbled so much that she dropped the keys. They both stooped at the same time, their hands reaching together for the keys. Serena's hand closed over them first, but at the touch of Leo's she reacted so violently that they fell chinking to the path again.

Leo retrieved them this time while she straightened, feeling ridiculous. 'Would you like me to open the door for you?' he asked, and she could hear the mockery edging his words.

'I can do it!' Practically snatching the keys from his hand, she managed to get the door open and stomped up the narrow stairs to her tiny first-floor flat.

To her discomfiture, Leo followed her into the kitchen and leant against the fridge while she filled the kettle and switched it on. He seemed to fill the room. Serena found that she was edging round him to pull down the cafetière and a couple of mugs, desperate in case she brushed against him by accident.

'Well?' she asked, retreating to the safety of the sink at the other end of the room while she waited for the kettle to boil. She ran some hot water into the cafetière to warm it and opened a new packet of freshly ground coffee. 'Are you going to tell me any more about this mysterious propositon of yours?'

'It's quite simple,' said Leo calmly. 'I need a fiancée.'

Serena's heart did a crazy somersault and she spilt ground coffee all over the worktop. With an exclamation of exasperation, she swept it into the sink with one hand and turned to face Leo very slowly. Her heart was thumping painfully against her ribs, making it hard to breathe. 'You need *what*?'

'A fiancée.'

'But I thought you didn't want to get married any more than I do!'

'I don't. I said I wanted a fiancée, not a wife.'

Completely lost, Serena put down the packet of coffee. 'I don't understand,' she said helplessly. She had expected Leo to ask her to do some extra cooking, perhaps a dinner party at his home—anything but this!

'I'll explain, but, if you're going to understand you'll need some of the background, so bear with me.' He straightened from the fridge and put his hands in his pockets, frowning down at his shoes as if wondering where to begin.

'You know I inherited my shares in the bank from my mother,' he said at last. 'What you probably don't know is that my parents were killed when I was sixteen. They'd always gone on about how I was destined to follow in my grandfather's footsteps but, as so often happens, they died before they had time to arrange the details. As a result my inheritance became part of an antiquated family trust. It meant I didn't receive anything until I was thirty.'

The kettle shrilled and Serena poured the boiling water into the cafetière, feeling strangely detached. 'I didn't know that,' she said carefully. 'I assumed you'd spent all your time at Erskine Brookes.'

'Far from it. The trust would have given me an allowance, of course, but if I'd taken that I'd have felt obliged to work at the bank. As it was, I wanted a taste of freedom before I took on my responsibilities. I'd grown up with the pressure of knowing what was expected of me.'

Leo was silent for a moment, as if remembering his childhood. 'Expectations are a hard thing for a child to bear. There were times when I hated the name Erskine Brookes. It was just assumed that it would be my life, and I wasn't sure that I wanted it. I began to think of the bank as a cage that I'd be locked into and never be able to leave.'

He paused. 'After my parents were killed, it was even worse. I had to keep on living up to expectations "because that's what your parents would have wanted". I finished school, like a good boy, and I went to university because that was expected of me, and then I realised that if I was ever going to have a taste of freedom it would have to be then. I was supposed to go straight into the bank and when I announced that I was going to work my way round the world instead my trustees effectively washed their hands of me.'

'Was freedom what you expected it to be?' asked Serena, curious in spite of herself.

Leo nodded. 'It was even better. I hadn't known until then what a sheltered, constricted upbringing I'd had. Suddenly I could do what I wanted, when I wanted, without the pressure of anyone's expectations but my own, without once having to think about that damned bank.' He looked up suddenly, his grey eyes very light and penetrating in his dark face. 'I suppose you're wondering what all this has to do with you?'

Serena nodded. 'It looks like being a long story,' she said, picking up the tray and carrying it through to the sitting-room. 'We might as well make ourselves comfortable. Go on,' she added as she set the tray down. 'What made you come back to the bank if you hated it so much?'

Leo watched her push down the plunger of the cafetière. 'Once I was free to live my own life, I didn't hate it any more,' he explained. 'I was happy for a while doing anything I could to keep me moving on but as I got older I began to want to get my teeth into something. I didn't want to settle down, but I *did* want a real challenge, and that's what Erskine Brookes is for me.

'I suppose there was a certain sense of inevitability about my return, too,' he went on. ' I don't think I ever lost sight of the fact that Erskine Brookes would be mine, and perhaps, deep down, I wanted to fulfil my parents' expectations after all. But I wanted to make it my bank, not my grandfather's, to do things my way, not his.' He took the mug Serena handed him and sat down opposite her on the sofa.

'So you decided to give up your freedom?'

'Only what was necessary,' said Leo. 'I knew that if I wanted to make a success of Erskine Brookes I'd have to compromise to a certain extent. I'd have to commit myself to the bank and to being settled in one place, but that was as far as I'd go.

'I still have the freedom of knowing I can give it all up if I choose to. I could get up tomorrow and go back to the way I was before, because I've got no personal commitments—no wife, no children, no ties at all. That's the real freedom that I still have, and it's the one freedom I'm not prepared to give up.'

'I see,' said Serena trying to ignore the empty feeling inside her. What difference did it make to her if he was determined to keep his freedom? She felt just the same. . .didn't she?

She cleared her throat. 'What happened when you came back to claim your inheritance?' she asked, keeping her voice deliberately light.

Leo gave one of his sudden smiles, the one that made her heart slam against her ribs. 'That makes it sound more dramatic than it was,' he said. 'Once I'd made the decision, I learnt what I could about banking in America, and when I was thirty I came home.

'I wasn't exactly welcomed with open arms! The trustees and the board of directors had got used to doing things their own way while I was away, and they were all very comfortable. They assumed that I'd let them carry on as before, and were horrified when they heard that I intended to take over the day-to-day running of the bank.'

He sighed. 'I've been struggling since then to break some of the old-fashioned notions they still cling to. You've seen how traditional the entrance hall is?' Serena nodded. 'Well, that's typical of their attitudes. They don't like change and they resist all my ideas on principle, but I have to play things very carefully.

Between them, they can still muster half the shares. I can't just kick them out.'

Getting to his feet, he prowled restlessly around the room, his hands cupped around the mug. 'I've been talking to the major shareholders of another bank about a merger. It's an unusual move but I think we need to expand, and the bank I have in mind, although small, has a number of high-net-worth individuals whose investments in various financial sectors complement our own.

'Naturally, there's resistance. This merger is a test of strength between me and my board. If it doesn't go through, they'll see it as a victory for tradition and I'll have to fight even harder in the future to make any changes at all. Frankly I'm prepared to do anything to make sure that it does go through.'

'So why can't you just bully them the way you do everyone else?' asked Serena, still utterly in the dark about her own role in all of this. 'What's the problem?'

'Redmayne and Co is a family-owned bank rather like Erskine Brookes, and Bill Redmayne, the chairman, wants to keep the bank in the family. His children, on the other hand, are anxious to realise some of their assets.'

'Well, if they want to sell, why can't you get them to persuade their father?'

'That was the original idea.' Leo paced back to where Serena was sitting on the worn sofa, sipping her coffee. 'Unfortunately, I've now discovered another problem.'

'Oh? What's that?'

He hesitated, then put his mug down on the coffee-table. 'The real problem is Noelle Redmayne.'

CHAPTER FOUR

SLOWLY, Serena lowered her mug. 'Noelle?' For some reason she didn't have to be told who Noelle was. The name suited her perfectly.

'You may have noticed her at lunch today,' said Leo. 'She's a very attractive girl.'

'I noticed,' said Serena coldly. 'I wouldn't have said that you were looking at her as if she was much of a problem either!'

'Noelle and her brother are my contacts with Bill Redmayne,' he said stiffly. 'Naturally, I've spent quite a bit of time entertaining them recently, to ensure that they don't lose interest or look elsewhere before I've had time to convince Bill and my board that a merger would be in all our interests.'

'I don't imagine that entertaining someone who looks like Noelle Redmayne is that much of a chore,' Serena remarked, remembering the way he had taken Noelle's arm to cross the road. 'Or are you going to tell me that your relationship is strictly businesslike?'

A muscle was beating in Leo's jaw and he looked as if he was holding on to his temper with difficulty. 'I'd like it to be,' he said curtly, frowning when Serena only raised her brows in eloquent disbelief. 'My priority at the moment is the merger,' he reminded her. 'Unfortunately, Noelle seems to have been misinterpreting my interest. She's taken to dropping hints about making it a personal merger as well as a financial one.'

'I'm surprised you haven't jumped at the suggestion,' said Serena acidly. 'You weren't exactly beating her off when I saw you!'

Leo shot her an angry look. 'In other circumstances it wouldn't be a problem, but I happen to know that what Noelle is really interested in is marriage.'

'And you don't want to tell her that you're not? You don't make any secret of it with anyone else!' Serena caught herself up guiltily as she heard the sharp note in her voice. Anyone would think she was jealous!

'I can't afford to alienate Noelle, especially not at the moment. I need her vote, and her influence with her father. Bill Redmayne dotes on her and if anyone can convince him to sell she can. If I tell her straight that there's no question of marriage she might withdraw her support; and if I wait until the merger's gone through I'll have Bill breathing down my neck and accusing me of leading his daughter on under false pretences.'

Determinedly reasonable now, Serena considered the matter. 'Yes, I can see it's a bit of a problem for you, ' she allowed reluctantly.

'What I need is to convince Noelle that she's wasting her time with me. I didn't see quite how I was going to do it without putting the matter bluntly, but the answer came to me when we were watching that video tonight.'

'I'm glad someone found it inspiring!'

'Actually, it was Richard's comment that set me thinking. You remember he said that we looked as if we were in love?'

Serena felt her cheeks grow hot. 'Richard doesn't know what he's talking about!'

'Of course not,' Leo agreed drily. 'But if he could be fooled, so could Noelle.'

Serena's green eyes were wary. 'What exactly are you suggesting?'

'I'm offering you a deal. I'll pay you a lump sum— shall we say five thousand pounds?—if you agree to act as my fiancée for as long as it takes for the merger to go through, and for Noelle to be convinced that I'm not available in the marriage stakes. It should only be for a matter of weeks—I think you'll find that it's a generous offer.'

'This merger must be very important to you,' said Serena slowly, still trying to take in what he had said.

'So is my freedom,' Leo told her. 'I want both.'

'And what you want you get?'

Silver eyes met challenging green ones across the coffee-table. 'Always,' he said.

There was a taut pause. Serena was the first to look away. 'Why are you asking me?'

'I'd have thought that was obvious. I could ask lots of girls but I couldn't rely on them not to get involved, whereas you've made it clear that you've no more interest in marriage than I have. At least you're honest about money being your priority. I'm offering you a chance to earn a substantial sum to put towards your savings. You're unlikely to get the opportunity to earn five thousand pounds that easily again.'

'I don't know that pretending to be in love with you would be that easy!' retorted Serena, riled by Leo's cool assurance that she would instantly fall in with his plan. And what a plan! Did he really think that she would get involved in such a callous pretence just for money?

She got to her feet, suddenly restless. She couldn't decide how she felt. Offended? Tempted? Ridiculously disappointed? It was the hollow feeling at the pit of her stomach that worried her most. She couldn't think of a single reason why she should feel disappointed that Leo had made her such a cold-blooded offer. Nor could she imagine why the thought of spending time with him should be so peculiarly tempting. A warning bell was ringing at the back of her mind, urging her to concentrate on feeling offended. It was much easier that way.

'You didn't seem to have any trouble pretending to

be in love with me at the wedding,' Leo pointed out, and Serena ruffled up at once.

'I wasn't pretending!'

Leo's brows rose in mock-astonishment. 'Surely you don't mean that you *were* in love with me?'

'You know perfectly well that I don't mean anything of the kind!' Serena snapped crossly. He had deliberately misunderstood her! 'I only kissed you because you provoked me. There was no question of pretence.'

'But look at how convincing you were!' said Leo. 'I don't think you'd have any difficulty at all in acting the part of an adoring fiancée, especially not when you knew you were getting paid for it.'

'Well, I think I would!' Yes, it was definitely easier to be angry than to wonder what it would be like if Leo wanted her to be a real fiancée instead of a hollow mockery. 'I'm afraid you'll have to find someone else to act out your little charade, Leo. I'm not interested.'

He didn't seem unduly downcast. 'You're much too headstrong, Serena. I've told you before that you might regret it.'

'Does that mean I'm out of a job?

'No, it means I'll give you the opportunity to think it over. You might change your mind.'

'I never change my mind!'

Leo smiled and drained his coffee, setting his mug down on the tray with a metallic clunk. We'll see,' he said.

'Serena?'

Serena struggled up against her pillows and squinted bleary-eyed at her alarm clock. Quarter past four in the morning. The insistent shrill of the telephone had dragged her out of a deep sleep filled with dreams of Leo.

'Madeleine?' she said sleepily, belatedly recognising her sister's choked voice. 'Madeleine, what's wrong?'

'It's Bobby.' Madeleine broke down in tears and it took long minutes before Serena could coax the whole story out of her. Bobby was her youngest nephew. She remembered him as a bright, sturdy little boy, but he was far from sturdy now. He had been rushed to hospital after collapsing without warning over the breakfast-table.

'The doctors are doing tests now,' Madeleine told her in a choked voice. 'But they don't know exactly what's wrong yet. They just keep saying that he's seriously ill and they'll have to wait and see. They think he's going to need special treatment, but I can't afford it. Chris cancelled the medical insurance when he ran out of money, and I haven't been able to afford to start again.' Her voice was rising into hysteria. 'What am I going to do, Serena? The hospital bills are going to be so expensive. . .'

It was some time before Serena could calm her distraught sister down. She knew from past experience that Madeleine responded best to a firm voice. 'You'll just have to bring him back to England. You're British, so Bobby will be entitled to treatment here.'

'It's too late for that,' said Madeleine tearfully. 'Even if I could afford the flights he's too sick to be moved far, and the best treatment for him is here—if I can pay for it.' Her voice began to wobble into panic again. 'And then there's the boys. What would I do with them? They've only just settled down after the move as it is, and I haven't been here long enough to know anyone I trust to look after them while I'm away. . .' She trailed off into sobs.

'I see.' Serena thought frantically. It never occurred to her that Madeleine was old enough to take responsibility for herself. Serena still thought of her sister as the timid little girl who had had to be protected from their father's cutting tongue.

When Chris had left her Madeleine had turned instinctively to her, and her only concern now was to help her as she had so many times before. If Madeleine needed money, money she should have—and Serena knew just how she could get it. Her heart might quail at the thought of taking Leo up on his offer, but she wouldn't hesitate if it would solve Madeleine's problem. . .and it would—or it might if she had the nerve to hold out for more money.

Her sister had told her how expensive medical bills could be, and she didn't think that the five thousand pounds Leo had offered would be enough. How highly did he value his freedom? It would be a gamble, but it was one she was prepared to take for Madeleine's sake.

'I think I've got the answer,' she said to her sister. 'You just concentrate on looking after Bobby and let me worry about the money. With any luck, I'll be able to send you some later today so you can make sure that he has the very best treatment.'

'But Serena, it's all going to be so expensive,' Madeleine protested in distress. 'And you haven't got any money either.'

Serena crossed her fingers. 'I will have tomorrow,' she said.

Wiping her palms nervously on her jeans, Serena hesitated outside Lindy's office. What if Leo had changed *his* mind? What if he had found someone else? What if he didn't want her to play the part after all? She had been stroppy enough last night. He might well have decided to look for someone more amenable. Or, worse, what if he had been joking all the time? What was she going to do then?

Oh, well, there was no point in dithering around out

here. Taking a deep breath, she pushed open the door and went in. She had prepared a careful excuse for Lindy's benefit, but it died on her lips as she saw Leo standing by his secretary's desk, a buff file open in his hands. He was obviously dictating something to her, but he broke off as the door opened, light eyes suddenly alert at the sight of Serena's tense face.

'Serena.' He closed the file very deliberately and dropped it on to the desk. 'Did you want to see me?'

'Yes,' said Serena baldly.

'You'd better come in.'

Lindy's face was bright with curiosity as Leo held open the door to his office and Serena walked straight past him without looking at him. Wordlessly, he followed her in and closed the door.

There was a silence. Serena stood irresolutely in the middle of the room. After she had put the phone down, she had lain awake rehearsing exactly what she was going to say but it didn't seem so easy with Leo's unsettling eyes on her face. His expression was inscrutable, and she watched, half resentful, half envious of his ability to keep his feelings hidden, as he walked past her and settled himself behind his desk, for all the world as if this were just another tedious business meeting.

'Don't you want to sit down?' he asked at last.

'Oh, yes. . .yes. . .' Oh, God, what if he *had* changed his mind? Flustered by his coolness, Serena perched on the edge of the straight-backed chair in front of his desk.

'Well?' said Leo with a trace of impatience when she still said nothing.

'It's about the offer you made me last night,' she blurted out at last.

'The one you refused?' His tone was light, but the silver eyes had sharpened and Serena took heart.

'Yes. I. . .I've changed my mind.'

'But I thought you never changed your mind,' Leo reminded her unfairly.

Serena's lips tightened. He obviously wasn't going to make this easy for her. 'Well, I've changed it now—for a price.'

'Surprise, surprise,' said Leo cynically, leaning back in his chair. 'And how much do you think you're worth, Serena?'

'Twenty thousand pounds.'

At least she had the satisfaction of breaking through that hateful assurance. Leo jerked abruptly forward, placing his palms flat down on his desk. '*What*?'

'Cash.' Serena fixed him with direct green eyes. There was no going back now. 'And five thousand pounds in advance.'

There was a blistering silence. 'I thought I'd met mercenary women before, but you give the concept a whole new meaning,' he said eventually. His voice was like a whiplash, and Serena had to force herself not to flinch. 'You said you valued yourself highly once, but I didn't realise you meant *that* highly! Extortionate would be a better word!'

'You can afford it,' said Serena doggedly. 'If the merger and your freedom are as important to you as you said they were, I'll be worth it.'

'You'd need to be very convincing to be worth that kind of money!'

She lifted her chin and looked him right in the eyes. 'I will be.'

'I wonder. . .' Leo pushed back his chair and came round to stand looking down at her with narrowed eyes, his hands thrust into his trouser pockets. His towering figure threatened to overwhelm her and, without thinking, Serena got uncertainly to her feet.

They faced each other, his dark, forceful features

only emphasised by the peculiar silver intensity of his eyes, and in direct contrast to Serena's vividness. Her eyes were very green, her chin tilted at a proud angle, and the light slanting through the window turned her hair to a rich, glinting copper.

She had secured it with a clasp at the nape of her neck. Almost impersonally, Leo unclipped it and spread the thick tumble of hair over her shoulders. Then his fingers drifted from her temple, down over the angle of her cheek to cup her throat between his hands while his thumbs traced the stubborn, deceptively fragile line of her jaw.

'I think you may have to prove to me just how convincing you can be,' he said softly.

Serena was having trouble breathing. Every sense quivered at his touch, so warm, so light, so disturbing. She knew she ought to say something, to remind him that this was a purely financial transaction, but she was pinned by that silver gaze and somehow all she could do was stare helplessly up at him while the words dried in her throat.

'If it weren't for the dollar signs clanging in those beautiful green eyes of yours, I might be tempted to take your word for it,' Leo went on in the same deep voice that seemed to vibrate down to her toes. 'As it is, I think I need some reassurance that I'm going to be getting my money's worth.'

Serena opened her mouth, but she never knew what she was going to say. It was too late by then, anyway. His lips were on hers, his hands tightening against her soft skin, and the office, the hostility, reality itself, swirled around her and dissolved in an explosion of delight.

It was like coming home at last. With a murmur of purely instinctive response, Serena leant into him and let her hands slide down his chest and around his back, revelling in the feel of his hard muscles through the soft cotton of his shirt.

Leo drew a brief, ragged breath and then, with a muttered exclamation, released her face to jerk her hard against him. His arm was tight around her, holding her close, while one hand tugged at her plain white T-shirt, dragging it free of her jeans so that he could explore the warm satin body beneath.

Serena gasped at the shocking, thrilling feeling of his skin against hers, the hard insistence of his hand moving up and down her spine, curving over her breast, exploring her hungrily while the irresistible pulse of excitement beat between them, slowly at first then gathering pace until it threatened to career beyond their control.

It was Leo who stopped it. Drugged with desire, Serena had forgotten everything but the throb of need inside her and, when he pulled down her T-shirt with a hand that was not quite steady and put her away from him she could only stare dazedly back at him while they both struggled to regain their breath.

'I think we've got a deal,' said Leo at last.

Deal? What deal? Serena's legs gave way abruptly and she collapsed back on to the chair. Her mind was still spinning with the exhilaration of that wonderful, terrifying, heart-stopping kiss and it was a physical effort to remember where she was and what she was doing.

Deal. Reality seeped back. Madeleine needed money and this was how she had agreed to get it. This was a purely financial transaction, a business arrangement. It had nothing whatsoever to do with love or desire or need and, whatever happened, she mustn't give Leo any reason to think otherwise.

She drew a shuddering breath and moistened her lips surreptitiously. 'What——?' Her voice was absurdly tight and high and she cleared her throat to start again. 'What happens now?'

Leo put his hands back in his pockets. She could feel him looking at her searchingly, but kept her own gaze fixed on his desk. In an odd, detached way, she concentrated on the details, on the dark green leather letter file, the slim gold fountain-pen, the pile of bound reports, on anything other than him. Her hair clasp was lying there as well and she retrieved it, clicking it mechanically between her fingers.

Muttering something under his beath, Leo wheeled away and paced over to the window. 'The first thing that happens is that we go shopping.'

'Shopping?' Surprise helped Serena to recover her expression. It was the last thing she had expected.

'You need some new clothes.'

'What for? What's wrong with what I've got on?'

He turned. 'Jeans and T-shirts don't give the right impression,' he said, and, unsought, the memory of his hand sliding beneath the white cotton shivered over Serena's skin. She swallowed and resumed her study of the desk. 'As far as I can gather, your wardrobe doesn't consist of anything else. You need smartening up.'

'I don't want to be smartened up!'

'What you want is immaterial,' said Leo flatly. 'If you're going to act as my fiancée, you've got to look the part.'

'I've got my red dress,' she reminded him, a little sulkily.

'You can hardly wear that every day.'

'Every day! How often am I going to have to do this?'

'As often as seems necessary,' he said in a cold voice. 'And at the price I'm paying you that will probably be very often.'

'I see.' Serena cast him a resentful glance. It wasn't

fair the way he could kiss her like that and carry on just as before. And why did he keep going on about the money? It had been his idea after all.

If it hadn't been for Bobby's illness there was no way she would have had anything to do with this crazy scheme, but she knew instinctively that it would be best not to admit as much to him. Far better for him to think of her as mercenary and calculating. That way he would carry on being thoroughly unpleasant and it would be much easier for *her* to remember just why she had agreed in the first place.

'Well, given that you *are* paying me perhaps we'd better agree on my duties before we go any further. Can you be a little more specific about what you're actually paying me *for*?'

'I'm paying you to be on display,' said Leo with brutal frankness. 'There's a cocktail party tonight I should go to; you can come with me. Noelle should be there so it will be a good chance to introduce you. After that, you'll have to be available in the evenings in case I need to take you to some function. Once word gets round that we're engaged, I've no doubt that you'll be included in some invitations.'

The prospect of sitting around waiting for a business-like summons to come and perform chilled Serena, but she thought of Bobby and gritted her teeth.

'How are we going to explain our engagement to friends?' she asked. 'People like Richard and Candace know exactly how I feel about marriage. They're not going to believe me if I suddenly turn round and announce that I'm going to marry you, are they?'

'They will if you tell them you've fallen madly in love with me.'

Serena's eyes shifted from his. 'And what happens when the merger goes through and we don't need to pretend any more? Do we just conveniently fall out of love?'

'Why not?' Leo shrugged. 'It happens all the time. If you prefer, you can tell your friends you changed your mind. Oh, I forgot, you never do, do you?'

She glowered at his sarcastic reminder of her attitude last night. 'Can't I at least tell Candace the truth?'

'No,' he said with flat finality. 'Surely twenty thousand pounds is enough to compensate for a bit of lost pride? *No one* is to know the arrangement we've made, is that clear?'

When Serena nodded reluctantly, he went on. 'It doesn't matter if I'm there or not, if you meet anyone else over the next few weeks you're to convince them that you're happily in love with me. And if I hear that anyone so much as suspects that you're not in fact intending to marry me, then the deal's off and you can wave goodbye to your twenty thousand pounds.

'I'll give you five thousand up front, since you insist, but the rest doesn't get paid until Bill Redmayne has agreed to the merger and Noelle has found someone else. You're going to earn every penny of that money, Serena,' he finished. 'I want you playing your role every minute of the time we're out together in public.'

'And in private?' She had to steel herself to ask, and Leo looked across at her with a faint, derisive smile.

'That, Serena, is up to you.'

'I can't go in there wearing jeans!'

Leo had swept her off straight after she had finished clearing up after lunch. They had already had a battle royal over her determination to carry on cooking. Leo seemed to think she should sit around all day waiting for his call, but Serena had been adamant. She simply didn't have the temperament to do nothing all day, she'd insisted, unable to tell him the real reason—that she had already arranged for the five thousand pounds to be sent to Madeleine, leaving her still in need of an income. Leo, of course, had drawn his own conclusions. 'Avarice must be your middle name!' he had sneered, but at least she had got her own way.

His chauffeur had dropped them in Bond Street and the name above the door Leo was heading for so purposefully made Serena's eyes widen in dismay. 'They won't let me through the door looking like this!'

'Oh, won't they?' Leo held open the door for her. 'They will when they discover they're going to transform you.'

As usual, Leo was right. Serena stood mutinously while he and an intimidatingly elegant saleswoman held up outfits against her and discussed her colouring as if she weren't there.

Dispatched to the fitting room with a whole pile of clothes, Serena began changing sulkily. When she sidled out in the first outfit—knee-length linen shorts and a silk top—the saleswoman helped her into a matching short-sleeved jacket and adjusted the fit on the shoulders with a finicky hand.

'This looks wonderful on you,' she gushed. 'Don't you agree, sir?'

'It's a distinct improvement,' agreed Leo, walking around Serena as if she were a dummy.

She twitched at the jacket. 'I can't wear this,' she hissed at him.

'Why not?'

'It's too. . .too *smart*. I'd never wear anything like this.'

'You will now,' said Leo.

They left the shop laden with discreetly elegant carrier bags rustling with tissue paper. Serena was appalled at the expense but Leo hardly glanced at the total before signing the sales voucher. He had bullied her into taking off her jeans and changing into a beautifully simple dress with short sleeves and a round neck. A plain cinnamon-brown with contrasting piping, it relied entirely on the cut and the material for its effect. She wore it with plain pumps, her hair falling loose down her back, and was astonished when she saw her reflection in the mirror.

Serena turned slowly, peering at herself doubtfully over her shoulder. She hardly recognised the stylishly sexy girl in the mirror.

Leo's reflection appeared behind hers. 'Do you like it?' he asked, tucking his wallet back into his jacket pocket.

'I don't know,' she said honestly to his reflection 'It doesn't look like me any more.'

'Oh, yes, it does.' Leo put his hands on her shoulders and made her stand still and look at herself properly. Serena was very conscious of the strength of his fingers through her jacket, through the silk pressing on to her skin. In the mirror, his eyes met hers. 'The jeans and the T-shirts are just a disguise that go with your prickles, Serena. Now you look like the passionate girl I recognise when I kiss you—so much more seductive than you ever want to admit.'

A slow shiver rippled down her spine. Ruffled, suddenly uncertain, she shrugged off his hands abruptly and turned from the mirror. 'You're wrong,' she said. 'The jeans are the real me. This——' she gestured down at the dress '—this is just the costume you've bought for the part I'm going to play.'

Something flickered in Leo's eyes, and then they shuttered. 'In that case, let's hope your performance is as convincing as the costume,' he said.

Outside, the May air was soft and fresh with the promise of an early summer and the sky above the pale grey London buildings was a high, pale blue. 'Where are we going now?' asked Serena, trotting to keep up with Leo as he set off down the pavement. The bags knocked against her long legs as she hurried after him.

'Burlington Arcade.'

'Am I allowed to ask why, or is this entire operation going to be conducted on a need-to-know basis?'

A corner of Leo's mouth twitched at her waspish tone. 'I'd have thought an intelligence officer like you would be able to work it out for yourself. What do we need to complete your cover?'

'Well, how am I supposed to——?' Serena broke off. 'A ring?' she asked in quite a different voice.

'A ring,' Leo confirmed. 'A ring fit for the girl I love.'

His words echoed in Serena's mind as they sat in the exclusive jeweller's looking at trays of fabulously sparkling rings. A ring fit for the girl Leo loved. Would he ever find one who meant more than his precious freedom?

She remembered what he had told her about his childhood, which his parents seemed to have viewed as a tedious but necessary training period for his position in Erskine Brookes. It wasn't surprising that he had broken free, or that, having discovered what freedom was, he should be so reluctant to give it up. She didn't blame him for his determination to keep his options open. Few people had the luxury of no commitments. If she didn't feel responsible for Madeleine, she wouldn't be here now.

Serena stared down at the rings, wondering what it would be like to be the girl who persuaded Leo that some things were worth more than freedom; what it would be like if this were for real, if she were sitting here beside Leo because he loved her and wanted to buy her a ring to prove it. The diamonds blurred suddenly beneath her gaze.

'What about this one?'

Pulling herself together, Serena took the ring Leo was holding out to her. It was a massive diamond encircled by smaller ones. She slipped it doubtfully on her third finger. 'Too ostentatious,' she decided.

The jeweller flinched and a shadow of exasperation crossed Leo's face. 'Have you got anything simpler?' he asked in a resigned tone. 'What are you doing?' he added to Serena as the jeweller removed himself with a martyred expression. She was wriggling in her chair, trying to tug down her skirt. She had been dismayed to find out how much shorter it seemed when she sat down.

'I'm not used to having quite so much leg on display,' she muttered.

Leo's eyes dropped to her slender knees. 'You've got wonderful legs,' he said. 'You should show them off more often instead of hiding them away the whole time.'

His gaze lifted to hers with a smile and, ridiculously, Serena blushed. The laughter-lines starring beneath his eyes were very pronounced and she felt as if she was seeing him with new clarity, noticing for the first time the texture of his skin, the very dark, very thick eyelashes and the way the hair grew from his forehead. The corner of his mouth twitched as his smile deepened and without warning her heart turned over, leaving her breathless and confused.

Then the jeweller was hovering before them again, presenting a velvet-covered tray of more exquisite rings. Serena bent her head over it with relief, glad of the excuse to hide her expression. What on earth was the matter with her? He had only smiled, for goodness' sake!

'This one.' Leo sounded quite decided as he picked up a ring and passed it to Serena. It was quite simple, a row of superb diamonds set in gold, with nothing to detract from their glittering purity.

'It's lovely,' Serena murmured, looking at it on her finger, unconscious of the wistful note in her voice. It fitted perfectly, almost as if it had been made for her. If only this were a gift of love, instead of a prop.

'We'll take it,' said Leo, an odd note in his own voice as he watched her face. He glanced up at the jeweller, who beamed benevolently from one to the other, obviously waiting for some demonstration of gratitude on Serena's part.

Sensing the air of anticipation, she looked up and realised that they were both watching her, the jeweller in an avuncular manner, Leo with a quizzical smile at the back of his eyes. He was waiting for her to play her part.

What would an ecstatic fiancée say if she had been given a ring like this for real? 'Thank you,' was all Serena could think of. Her voice was husky as she leant across and kissed Leo on the cheek. His skin smelt clean and warm, firm beneath her lips. Before she could draw back, Leo lifted his hand to turn her face tenderly so that he could find her lips with his own, and for an instant it was as if they forgot they were playing roles. It was only a brief kiss, but so sweet that, stupidly, tears shimmered in her eyes as he let her go.

CHAPTER FIVE

THE diamonds glittering on her finger kept catching at the edge of Serena's vision as she let herself into her flat. Leo had put her in a taxi, tossed the carrier bags in after her and told her to go home and change.

'Be back at the bank at six o'clock,' he had ordered before striding off down the pavement without so much as a backward look to see if she was all right. 'We'll go on to the cocktail party together.'

Serena had given the taxi driver her address in a listless voice, and slumped back into her seat as it pulled out into the Piccadilly traffic. What had she expected? A loving farewell? The kiss they had shared in the jeweller's had been so unexpectedly tender that she was in grave danger of forgetting that they were just playing an elaborate charade.

Leo hadn't forgotten. He had turned away so that the jeweller could murmur to him discreetly about the price and when he had come back the familiar, shuttered expression had been firmly back in place. Taking her arm in a firm grasp, he had marched her out of the shop and replied to her feeble attempts at conversation in brusque monosyllables until he had managed to hail the taxi.

Serena threw the carrier bags on to her bed and went into the kitchen to make herself a cup of tea, prowling edgily around the room while she waited for the kettle to boil. It had all seemed so easy this morning when Madeleine's phone call had made her change her mind about Leo's offer. The trouble was that it *wasn't* easy, and Serena had a nasty feeling that it was only going to get more difficult.

If only he hadn't kissed her. Things would be so much easier if he hadn't, and a whole lot less difficult if her treacherous body didn't betray her by responding every time he touched her. Serena sighed and she fished the tea-bag out of the mug, and the diamonds on her finger flashed a reminder that it was too late to change her mind now.

The doorman didn't recognise her when she walked into the bank just before six. Desperate to take her mind off Leo and the way she had felt when he had kissed her, Serena had washed her hair and the shining coppery waves bounced over her shoulders as she walked up the steps. She wore a navy and white suit with a short, round-necked jacket and a knee-length skirt, and the bold gilt buttons glinted in the light. It was only when she smiled at him that the doorman recognised the fiercely practical cook in the lovely, elegant girl standing before him, and his jaw dropped.

'Gawd, I didn't recognise you! I thought you were a model, or something!'

Serena grinned. 'No, it's just me, Fred.'

'Not cooking tonight, then?'

'No.' She hesitated. 'I. . . Actually, I've come to meet Mr Kerslake.'

'Oh.' Fred managed to invest it with at least five syllables. Whistling soundlessly, he watched with undisguised curiosity as Serena walked with assumed nonchalance over to the lifts. The news would be all over the bank the next day, she realised fatalistically.

Leo was just giving some final notes to Lindy when she walked into the office. In spite of her determination not to let him affect her any more, her heart gave a great bound at the sight of him. He looked up and his face lightened with a welcoming smile that Serena found herself returning almost shyly before she remembered that he was only acting. He wasn't really pleased to see her.

A quivering sigh from the desk made them both look round in surprise. Lindy was dabbing at her eyes with a tissue. 'I just think it's so romantic,' she apologised weepily.

'What is?' Serena looked at her blankly.

'I've just been telling Lindy our good news,' said Leo, recalling her to her role with a distinct edge to his voice.

'I'm so happy for you,' Lindy added tremulously.

'Oh—er—thank you,' said Serena awkwardly.

'Come on, darling, we'd better go.' Leo propelled her out of the room with a firm hand at her back. 'You'll have to do better than that,' he said acidly as he closed the door behind them.

'Well, *I* don't know how you behave when you're engaged,' grumbled Serena, trotting to keep up with his long strides along the corridor.

'All you had to do was look happy to see me!'

'I suppose you wanted me to kiss you again?' she snapped, determined not to admit even to herself— particularly not to herself—that she *had* been happy to see him.

'That would have been a nice touch,' said Leo evenly.

'I can hardly spend my whole time flinging myself into your arms!'

Leo rolled his eyes heavenwards. 'It's not as if I'm asking you to take part in an orgy,' he told her with exaggerated patience. 'A little gesture of affection every now and then is all that's required.'

'I've said I'll do my best and I will,' said Serena defensively as the lift slid downwards. 'But I'm a cook, not an actress. Don't expect an Oscar-winning performance!'

'Oh, I don't know,' Leo returned with a sardonic look. 'You deserved a nomination at least for the performance you put on in the jeweller's this afternoon. That kiss was really very convincing. Old Bagshott was quite won over. He even told me what a lucky man I was!'

Serena refused to meet his gaze. She could feel the treacherous colour stealing up her throat at the reminder of that kiss. 'That's what you wanted, wasn't it? What are you complaining about?'

'I'm not complaining. I'm just pointing out that if you could do it then you can do it now. Noelle will be there this evening, so it's important that you put on an equally convincing performance for her.' The doors opened and they stepped out into the entrance hall. Leo lowered his tone. 'There will also be a number of important people there, so I'd be grateful if you could keep that sharp tongue of yours between your teeth. Perhaps you could try and live up to your name a little more than you do usually? A bit of sweetness and serenity would make a nice change!'

Serena grumbled all the way to the cocktail party which was being held at one of the smarter London hotels. 'I can't bear these affairs. Standing around and making small talk to a lot of strangers always seems a completely pointless exercise.'

'It may be pointless for you,' said Leo, 'but for me it's a very useful way of making contact with people I may need to deal with in the future. All you have to do is stand next to me and look decorative.' He cast her a speculative, sidelong look in the back of the car. 'And you do look surprisingly decorative this evening. In fact,' he added slowly, 'you look beautiful.'

Serena glanced at him uncertainly and found that she

couldn't look away. There was an odd expression in Leo's eyes and for some reason her heart began to thud, slowly and painfully, against her ribs.

'Here we are, sir.' The chauffeur drew up outside the hotel and got out to open the door for Serena, who drew a rather unsteady breath and tried to pull herself together.

Even so, she was burningly conscious of Leo's hand resting possessively against her back as they walked into the reception. He was obviously a well-known figure, able to move easily from group to group, and for the first time she acknowledged the charismatic charm that she had been at such pains to deny—because denying it made it much easier to resist.

With a small frisson she realised how reassuring it was to be with someone like Leo, to be able to rely on him to lead the conversation if necessary, knowing that, whatever happened, he would know what to say and do. For Serena, used to battling on by herself, it was an unusual and alarmingly comforting feeling.

At first she felt awkward and out of place but as she got used to the frank admiration of his colleagues and associates she began to relax, and even to enjoy herself. There was no doubting that clothes made a difference—or was it being with Leo? Impatient of superficiality and, since Alex, wary of men, Serena had always shunned attention before but now, forced into the limelight with Leo's tall, reassuring presence by her side, she discovered that she didn't dislike it quite as much as she'd thought she would.

Gradually, her natural warmth and wit began to unfurl; spiced with astringency, they made an intriguing combination with her unfashionable directness. Every now and then she would feel the warning pressure of Leo's hand if she was going too far, and occasionally she would catch him watching her with an expression that was half startled, half amused, as if he was taken aback by the transformation taking place in front of his eyes.

He kept her by his side, a hand at her waist or beneath her elbow. Serena was aware of him always. She wondered if he was waiting for her to produce some gesture of lover-like affection. It hardly seemed appropriate to turn and kiss him in these surroundings, but she was unsettled by how clearly she could imagine it. Her lips tingled as if they were already touching his skin and the thought of relaxing against him was terrifyingly vivid. His arm would slip round her and hold her close, and she would be anchored to the solid security of his body.

She took a slug of her wine in an attempt to dispel the image and stiffened as she recognised an all too familiar face through a gap in the crowds. Candace was staring at her in astonishment and as Serena watched in consternation she turned to Richard and tugged at his sleeve.

Serena's heart sank and her hand stole quite instinctively into Leo's. She had been dreading facing Candace. Her friend might be fluffy-headed at times, but she could also on occasion be alarmingly sharp where Serena was concerned. Serena had been hoping that she could somehow get away without telling her at all. She certainly hadn't been expecting to come across her *here*!

At the convulsive pressure of her hand, Leo glanced down at her in surprise. 'Candace and Richard have seen us,' she muttered out of the corner of her mouth.

Murmuring an excuse, he detached them from the group with practised charm. 'It had to happen some time,' he said as he drew her to meet Candace and Richard halfway. 'It might as well be now.'

'Serena!' Candace swept down on her, bearing

Richard in her wake. 'I've been standing there saying, That's Serena. . .no, it can't be, but it *is* you! You look fantastic!'

Serena suddenly realised that her hand was still in Leo's and tried to withdraw it, but he kept her in a firm grasp. 'Hello, Candace,' she said feebly. 'What are you doing here?'

'Oh, Richard has to come along to all these dos and chat up other brokers. They're usually deadly, but this one's not too bad.' Candace kissed Leo with undisguised curiosity. 'More to the point, what are *you* doing here, Serena? I thought you hated this kind of thing?'

'She's going to get used to it,' Leo answered for her, releasing Serena's hand to put his arm around her waist and draw her close. 'Aren't you, darling?'

Candace's eyes bulged at the endearment and she looked from Leo to Serena in eager anticipation. 'When did all this happen?' she demanded.

'Last night,' said Leo smoothly, and, taking Serena's left hand, he showed Candace the ring. 'You'll be glad to know that your matchmaking plans are working out already, Candace.'

'I knew it!' Candace's shriek of delight caused a momentary break in the buzz of conversation as heads turned around the room to see what all the excitement was about. 'I *knew* it!' Unable to contain herself, she threw herself at Leo and Serena, enveloping them in hugs. 'I always knew that one day you'd just meet someone, Serena, and that would be that! And didn't I say Leo would be perfect for you? Of course, it was obvious last night that you were in love.'

'It was?' said Serena faintly.

'Oh, yes,' Candace assured her. 'Even Richard noticed the way you kept on looking at each other when the other one wasn't watching.'

Serena squirmed, but Leo only tightened his arm

about her. 'That was very astute of you,' he said with some dryness. 'We didn't know ourselves until I took Serena home.'

'Oh, we knew *you* didn't know,' Candace told him kindly. 'Richard actually said to me after you left, When do you think those two are going to realise they're in love? Didn't you, darling? But we never thought it would be quite so soon!' She hugged Serena again. 'Oh, I'm so happy for you!'

'Congratulations!' said Richard, finally managing to get a word in edgeways as his wife paused for breath. He wrung Leo's hand and kissed Serena warmly on the cheek. 'It's always nice to have one's theories confirmed so promptly!'

Candace had pounced on the ring. 'Serena! It's beautiful!' She looked at her friend with awe and not a little envy. 'You lucky thing! You must be so happy!'

Leo tensed almost imperceptibly, but Serena was so attuned to him that he might as well have jumped. This was her biggest test yet. If she could convince Candace, she could convince anyone. 'Yes, yes, I am,' she agreed a little huskily. 'It just takes a little getting used to.'

At least that seemed to be the right thing to say. 'I can imagine!' said Candace, and Serena felt Leo relax. 'Falling in love when you're not expecting it knocks you for six, doesn't it?'

'I can't believe it's all happened in the last twenty-four hours,' Serena confessed with perfect honesty. Had Madeleine's phone call really only been last night? She seemed to have been playing this charade forever.

'Never mind,' Candace was saying. 'You'll get used to it, just like I did.' She took Serena's arm and drew her aside, away from the safe shelter of Leo's body, leaving Leo and Richard talking together. 'Now, I want to know *all* about it. I always knew that when you finally fell in love it would be with a bang. When was the big moment when you realised you were in love with Leo? The first time he kissed you?'

Serena felt something cold settle at the pit of her stomach and the room seemed to rock around her. She closed her eyes briefly; when she opened them again, her surroundings had settled, and she shook her head to clear it of the peculiar sensation.

She must have had too much to drink. For one awful moment there she had felt as if this charade was for real and an inexplicable answer had trembled on her lips. . .but there was no question of her being in love with Leo. Absolutely, definitely not. She was letting the role get to her, that was all. Perhaps she was a better actress than she had thought.

'Serena?' Candace was looking at her curiously.

Belatedly, Serena realised that she still hadn't answered her question. 'I. . .yes, I think it was then.'

'Poor Serena,' laughed Candace, not seeming to find her behaviour the slightest bit odd. 'You *have* got it bad! What about you, Leo?' she called, turning to make him break off his conversation with Richard and lift one enquiring eyebrow. 'When did you realise you were in love with Serena?'

He looked at Serena, who was regarding him with apprehensive green eyes. 'The first time I laid eyes on her,' he said softly.

Anyone would think he had been rehearsing, Serena thought with a dull sense of misery.

'She was walking up the aisle behind you and I turned and our eyes met.' He ran a finger caressingly down her cheek. 'Do you remember that, Serena?'

To her horror, Serena felt herself blush. 'I remember,' she muttered. She was convinced that his finger had left a burning trail down her face and that it was throbbing there for everyone to see.

'Will you excuse us, Candace?' said Leo, putting his

arm around her, for all the world a possessive fiancé.
'There's someone over here I want Serena to meet.

'You look a bit odd,' he went on in an undertone as
he led her across the room, and she could almost swear
there was real concern in his voice. 'Are you all right?'

'Of course,' she said brightly. She could hardly admit
that she had been shaken off balance by the brief touch
of one of his fingers! 'I'm just a bit tired, that's all. I
didn't get much sleep last night, thinking about your
offer.'

'And calculating how much you could get out of me?'
ne added for her, suddenly harsh, as if she had just
reminded him of something he had almost forgotten.

She *had* done that, Serena realised a little guiltily.
'Who are we going to see?' she asked, deciding that it
was better to ignore the whole issue.

'Oliver Redmayne—Noelle's brother—so be careful
what you say, and for God's sake be nice.'

Oliver Redmayne was tall and blond, like his sister.
He was very good-looking too, with an air of rather
affected charm and blue eyes which roved over Serena
appreciatively. 'I hear congratulations are in order,' he
said when Leo had introduced her. 'The whole room's
buzzing with the news! You've caught us all on the hop,
Leo. We all thought you were a confirmed bachelor.'

'I used to think so too,' said Leo. Serena thought his
tone was surprisingly cool considering that Oliver was
so important to the success of his precious merger.

'So what made you change your mind?' Oliver's eyes
slid over Serena's curves and down her legs and his
smile widened. 'Or can I guess?'

Leo's hand tightened suddenly at Serena's waist.
'Serena is a very special girl,' was all he said.

'So special that you really shouldn't be hogging her
all to yourself,' Oliver told him, taking Serena's hand
with practised charm. 'You go and circulate, Leo, and

I'll look after Serena for you. I've got a good mind to try and persuade her not to throw herself away on riff-raff like you!'

Leo's smile was perfunctory at best. He hesitated, looking down at Serena. 'Will you be all right with Oliver?' he asked. 'There are a couple of people I need to have a word with and it will just be boring business for you.'

'I'll be fine,' said Serena, tilting her chin. She would have died rather than admit that she would rather stay with him.

'I'll be back in a few minutes.' Leo touched her cheek fleetingly. 'Don't take Oliver too seriously, will you?'

'Well, well!' said Oliver as Leo was swallowed by the crowd. 'Leo Kerslake smitten at last! There'll be teeth gnashing all over London tonight, you mark my words. I know of several ladies who will have their noses put severely out of joint, having stuck with Leo for ages in the hope of enticing him to the altar only to decide like all the others that he was allergic to the whole idea.

'I warned my dear sister that she was wasting her time, and it seems I was right for entirely the wrong reasons! He was obviously just holding out for the best, and I can't say I blame him.' His hand smoothed down Serena's back. 'You look stunning. No wonder Leo's been keeping you to himself.'

When Leo came anywhere near her, Serena strummed with awareness. She hardly noticed Oliver's caressing hand.

Once Oliver realised that she wasn't going to fall for his practised lines he dropped his affection and they got on surprisingly well. He would be amusingly irreverent and kept her entertained with an inexhaustible flow of gossip. Serena encouraged him to talk about himself too, thinking that would be easier than fending off questions about her relationship with Leo.

'I'm a terrible disappointment to my father,' he confessed. 'He can't understand why I want Redmayne and Co to merge with Erskine Brookes. He thinks I should be fighting to keep the bank in the family so that I can hand it on to my son one day.'

'Don't you want that?'

'God, no!' exclaimed Oliver, horrified. 'I wouldn't subject a child of mine to a lifetime's subservience to Redmayne and Co!'

'So you won't continue working with Leo if your father agrees to the merger?'

Oliver grinned. 'I can't wait to shake the dust of banking from my feet! I want to try something completely different. In spite of all appearances to the contrary, I'm a country boy at heart. We've an estate in Yorkshire, and I've often thought about opening a sort of country club place—very classy, of course—up there, not too far from Leeds and Sheffield.'

'You could do that anyway, couldn't you?' Serena asked. She had been trying to spot Leo surreptitiously, but he seemed to have completely disappeared. 'With a bank in the family, you can't be exactly purse-pinched!'

'You'd be surprised,' said Oliver glumly. 'The old man won't hear of the idea, and all my own money is tied up in bank shares. As far as I can see they're worthless at the moment, but if we merge with Erskine Brookes they'll go through the roof. The sooner the merger takes place, the sooner I can realise my assets and start looking for a suitable place. At the moment, my hands are tied. I can't do anything until I've got some cash behind me.'

'I can understand that,' sighed Serena, thinking of her own ambitions which had been shelved until she could sort out Madeleine's problems.

'You won't have to worry about money ever again when you marry Leo.'

'What about your sister?' she asked quickly to change the subject. 'Does she want to stay with the bank?'

'To tell you the honest truth, Serena, I think she wanted Leo Kerslake more than the merger, but now he's out of the running I dare say she'll be happy, like me, to settle for the cash.'

At that moment a man in front of Serena stepped back to let someone pass, and through the gap she caught sight of Leo on the far side of the room. His dark head was bent down to a sleek blonde one and Serena's eyes narrowed as he turned slightly and she recognised his companion. It was Noelle Redmayne.

So much for 'boring business'!

The other girl looked stunning in a daringly cut white dress that Serena would certainly never have had the nerve to wear. Oliver was talking on, but Serena couldn't concentrate on what he was saying. She kept seeing Leo and Noelle out of the corner of her eye. Glancing over again, she saw Noelle lay a perfectly manicured hand on Leo's arm and lean closer to whisper something in his ear that made him smile. He murmured something in reply and Noelle let out a trill of laughter.

Serena's fingers tightened on her glass. She wanted to stalk over to them and slap Noelle's hand from his arm. She wanted to wipe that smug smile from her face and remind Leo that he was supposed to be engaged to *her*. Her green eyes blazed and, almost as if he had felt the full force of her glare, Leo glanced across and caught her watching him.

Very deliberately, Serena turned to Oliver with a brilliant smile that made him blink visibly. She had never flirted in her life before, but jealous fury gave her inspiration and she proceeded to dazzle Oliver with a skill that surprised herself. She laughed up at him, sent him long, suggestive looks under her lashes, let her fingers trail down his arm. Oliver, initially bemused by her abrupt change of attitude, was delighted to reciprocate.

The next minute Leo was bearing down on them, Noelle in tow, and Serena was gratified to see that he was looking very grim. 'Oh, hello,' she said airily as if noticing him for the first time. 'Back already?'

'I trust I'm not interrupting anything?' Leo bit out.

'Interrupting?' She opened her eyes at him in innocent astonishment. 'Of course not! Oliver's been looking after me,' she told him brightly, and bestowed another sparkling smile on Oliver, who was looking wry. 'I've been having a lovely time.'

Leo's black look deepened. 'I don't think you've met Noelle Redmayne, have you?' he said with an effort to sound pleasant that sat oddly with his expression. 'Noelle, this is my fiancée, Serena Sweeting.'

'What a pretty name!' said Noelle with a light laugh. Her eyes were as blue as Oliver's, but where his were warm hers were very, very cold. 'Are you as serene and sweet as you sound?'

Serena could play at that game too. Taking Leo's arm ostentatiously between both her hands, she leant her cheek whimsically against his shoulder. 'I don't know about that, but Leo thinks I'm sweet, don't you, darling?'

A muscle was beating in Leo's jaw. 'Some of the time,' he said. He looked as if he was already regretting having introduced the two girls, who were eyeing each other with acute dislike.

'Leo's been telling me you've had quite a whirlwind romance,' Noelle went on sweetly, managing somehow to imply that Leo was in the habit of confiding all his deepest secrets to her and that this was just one of many. 'It's very brave of you to get engaged when you've known each other such a short time.'

It was plain to Serena that Noelle was pinning her hopes on such a short-lived—and patently unsuitable— relationship foundering, and that she had by no means given up her hopes of Leo yet.

'Do you think so?' she said, equally saccharine. 'It doesn't seem brave at all to me. It just seems absolutely right. After all, how long does it take to fall in love?' She simpered up at Leo, who was looking wooden, and twirled her hand so that Noelle could get a good look at her engagement ring. 'I knew the moment I saw Leo that he was the man for me. Now it feels as if we've known each other *forever*. Don't you feel like that, darling?' she added provocatively.

'Sometimes,' said Leo with a distinctly warning glance. 'And sometimes I feel as if I hardly know you at all!'

'We've got the rest of our lives to get to know each other,' Serena reminded him soulfully. 'In every way,' she added, with one of the suggestive looks she had been practising on Oliver for Noelle's benefit.

Peeping a glance at the other girl, she was delighted to see that she was looking daggers. Well, it wouldn't do any harm to underline the point, she thought, and reached up to kiss Leo's ear before nestling close to him. She was beginning to enjoy her role. 'Leo's told me so much about you, Noelle. You *must* come to the wedding.'

Noelle didn't seem particularly grateful for the invitation. 'Oliver, are you ready?' she asked abruptly. 'We really should be going.'

'Oh, must you?' said Serena with mock-regret. She was cock-a-hoop at having been able to put Noelle so firmly in her place.

'And so must we,' put in Leo firmly before she could go any further. 'Goodbye, Oliver. . .and I'll see you tomorrow, then, Noelle?'

Noelle shot Serena a triumphant look. 'I'll look forward to it,' she cooed, with a secret, shared smile that pointedly excluded Serena, and, taking Oliver's arm she swayed off into the crowd.

CHAPTER SIX

SERENA was livid. 'What do you mean, you'll see her tomorrow?' she demanded as Leo practically dragged her from the room.

'I've got some business matters to discuss with her,' he said, with a look that boded no good for when they were alone, but Serena was too angry too care.

'Oh, yes? Like the "boring business" you had to deal with this evening? I can guess what business *that* was!'

'I don't know what you're talking about,' he said coldly.

'Oh, come on, Leo! I saw you whispering in her ear, and it certainly wasn't about the exchange rate.'

Leo ignored her while he arranged for his chauffeur to be paged, and when he turned back to her his jaw was clenched with the effort of keeping his temper under control. 'Look, I've already explained how important it is to keep Noelle sweet.'

'There's a difference between keeping her sweet and pouring on the treacle. I felt sick just watching you!'

'Don't be ridiculous!' he snapped, striding out through the doors to wait for the car outside.

'I'm not being ridiculous. You made me look a complete fool!'

'I made *you* look a fool?' uttered Leo with a mirthless crack of laughter. 'That's a good one! How do you think you made me look with that childish performance you just put on? "Leo thinks I'm sweet",' he mimicked her savagely. 'Sweet! Hah! You're about as sweet as a lemon!'

'You were the one who wanted me to live up to my

100

name,' Serena reminded him furiously. 'You went on and on and on about behaving like a besotted fiancée, so that's what I did. And what's more I'd just convinced Noelle that she didn't stand a chance when you spoilt everything by making an assignation with her tomorrow!'

'It's not an assignation.' Leo contained himself long enough for them to get into the back of the car and make sure that the panel dividing them from the chauffeur was firmly closed. 'Noelle's absolutely vital to the merger. The last thing I want is to antagonise her, which is precisely what you did. All I wanted to do was discourage her from taking a personal interest in me. Now, thanks to you, I'm going to have to work even harder to keep her on my side.'

'You weren't doing a very good job of discouraging her when I saw you,' retorted Serena, throwing herself back against the seat and folding her arms crossly. 'Whispering sweet nothings in her ear, letting her fondle you as if she owned you. . .you want to have your cake and eat it, don't you? Have Noelle hanging on your every word, but not in any position to cramp your precious freedom!'

'You're a fine one to talk about fondling,' snarled Leo. 'You and Oliver could hardly keep your hands off each other. I thought you didn't like men?'

'Only some,' said Serena with a nasty look. 'I thought Oliver was charming.'

'That was obvious. I don't see how you can possibly imagine you convinced Noelle about anything when she and the rest of the room could see you flirting unashamedly with her brother. Then you made things worse with that revolting performance. Do you think Noelle really believes I'd fall in love with someone who simpered and gushed like that?'

'I'm sure she doesn't—thanks to you. You weren't

exactly a model of lover-like behaviour. It was like cuddling up to a wooden block!'

A muscle was hammering in Leo's temple. 'I'd have thought it was quite natural for me to be unresponsive then. I'm hardly likely to have been overjoyed at the sight of my fiancée all over another man. If I'd really been in love with you, I'd have taken him outside and punched him!'

'I wasn't all over him,' denied Serena haughtily. She had no intention of telling him that he only reason she had flirted with Oliver was that she had seen *him* all over Noelle. That sounded much too much like jealousy and might give Leo quite the wrong idea. 'We were talking, that's all. I didn't have much choice after you dumped me with him and swanned off to chat up Noelle. You were the one who told me to be nice to him, after all.'

'I didn't mean you to be that nice!'

Serena gave up. There was obviously no point in arguing with him in this mood. Rigid with temper, she stared vengefully out of her window. He was impossible! She had acted exactly as instructed, and fine thanks she got for it!

The rest of the journey passed in simmering silence. When they reached her flat, Serena was out of the car before the chauffeur had a chance to open his own door. As she stalked up the path, she heard Leo ask him to wait.

'There's absolutely no need to see me to my door,' she said icily when he followed her.

'Unfortunately there is. In spite of not being able to hear anything, it must have been patently obvious to Harry that we were having an almighty row in the back. I want him to be able to report to anyone who asks tomorrow that we've made it up.'

'Who on earth is going to be interested?' asked

Serena contemptuously, searching for her keys in her bag.

'You'd be surprised. Between them, Lindy, Harry and Fred will make sure that the entire bank knows that we're engaged tomorrow, and, human nature being what it is, most of them will want to know details. I'm not having Harry confiding to everyone that the whole thing seems to be off already.'

'If you're so anxious to impress Harry, stand at the gate and shout "sorry",' Serena suggested acidly. Where *were* her keys?

'That's not how lovers make up, Serena, and you know it.'

'Well, have you got a better idea?'

'Yes,' he said. 'I'm going to kiss you.'

Serena's fingers closed convulsively over her keys at last. Her head jerked up and she glared at him. 'Like hell you are!'

'If you don't like it, you'd better just close your eyes and think of the money,' advised Leo, calmly removing her bag from her suddenly nerveless hands and dropping it to the ground, where it landed with a soft thud on the step. 'I'm sure you do that anyway.'

'I don't want to kiss you,' said Serena breathlessly, nearly tripping over the bag as she backed up the step away from him.

'That's too bad,' said Leo, following her up the step until she was pinned helplessly against the door, green eyes huge and defiant. 'Because I'm going to kiss you anyway and, for Harry's benefit, *you* are going to respond.'

'I won't!' she protested, but Leo only pulled her ruthlessly into his arms and before she knew what was happening his mouth was on hers and he was kissing her—the hard, punishing kiss of man pushed too far.

Serena rammed her hands against his chest as if to

ward off the wave of temptation that threatened to
engulf her, but it was useless. It came rolling over her,
ignoring her puny efforts to resist, sweeping her along
in a dizzying rush of sensation, and as if sensing the
change in her Leo relaxed his grip.

'Damn you, Serena,' he muttered, sliding one hand
up to wrap it in the soft, shining mass of hair. 'Damn
you,' he said again, even as his mouth found hers once
more and a tide of indescribable sweetness caught them
both unawares. Swirling them along in a breathless
rush, it swamped the jealousy and the anger and the
bitter words dissolving them in deep pools of gathering
desire.

Helpless before its whirling force, intoxicated by the
feel of his lips moving so persuasively against her own
and the delicate, tantalising exploration of his tongue,
Serena abandoned any attempt to push him away.
Instead, she melted against him, offering him her
warmth. Her fingers fumbled to unbutton his jacket
and stole beneath, spreading luxuriously over the steely
strength of his body.

Leo gathered her closer while desire whispered its
urgent message between them, swirling through the
sweetness to echo along their veins. Serena could feel
it flickering into fire, feeding on the excitement of Leo's
hands roaming over her body and the electrifying
delight of their kisses, and she murmured something
that might have been a plea or a protest.

He must have heard it as a protest for he released
her reluctantly, letting his hands slide slowly from her
tousled hair as he looked down at her with an
expression in his eyes she had never seen before. He
had been as unprepared as she for that explosion of
passion, she realised shakily.

'I hope you think Harry will have got the message by
now,' she said unsteadily.

'I'm sure he will.' Leo hesitated, as if he was about to say something else, but then changed his mind abruptly. 'I'll see you tomorrow,' was all he said, and strode back to the car, leaving Serena still leaning weakly against the door.

Leo was right about the speed with which the news of their supposed engagement spread round the bank. An extraordinary number of people managed to find an excuse to drop into the kitchen the next day to discover whether the intriguing rumour was true, and by the time the tenth secretary had admired her ring and told her enviously how lucky she was Serena's temper was beginning to get a little frayed. It was all right for Leo. He could hide himself in meetings all day, and anyway, no one would dare ask him to his face.

He didn't appear at lunch. Probably out slobbering over Noelle, Serena realised, washing up with a sort of controlled savagery. If it weren't for Madeleine, she would tell him just what he could do with his 'engagement'!

Unfortunately, Madeleine had rung just as she had let herself into the flat last night and, hearing her sister's distress, Serena had known that there was no way she could jeopardise the financial security she had offered. Bobby was still very ill, but the money she had transferred that morning would be one thing off Madeleine's mind for a while.

She was preparing a vichyssoise for lunch the next day when Leo finally deigned to remember her existence. He came into the kitchen just as she was pouring the leeks and potatoes into the blender. As always the sight of him tightened her stomach and clogged the breath in her throat, and she put the saucepan down abruptly on the worktop.

'Did you and Noelle have a good lunch?' she asked waspishly.

'Delicious, thank you, Serena,' said Leo, refusing to rise to the bait. 'You'll be glad to know that Oliver came along too, to act as chaperon.'

Serena hunched a sulky shoulder. 'I don't care what you do with Noelle.'

'That wasn't the impression you gave last night.' Leo strolled over to inspect the saucepan. 'What's this?'

'Soup,' she said shortly, whisking it away and pouring the rest of the leeks into the blender. 'If you want to make a fool of yourself over Noelle, that's fine by me — as long as you don't make me look ridiculous as well.'

Leo opened his mouth to reply, but she forestalled him by switching on the blender. 'Sorry?' she shouted provocatively over the noise.

He waited with infuriating calm until she was forced to turn it off. 'I thought you might like to know that we've made some progress. Noelle's persuaded her father to meet me socially. If he approves of me he says he might consider a formal meeting, so with any luck the end of our charade might be in sight sooner than I thought. As soon as Bill Redmayne agrees to the merger, we can call the whole thing off.'

'The sooner the better,' grumbled Serena. 'I've had the entire bank trooping through the kitchen this morning wanting to know what you're really like — oh, don't worry, I didn't tell them! I was lucky to get any cooking done at all.'

'You were the one who wanted to carry on working,' Leo reminded her, unmoved.

'I wanted to cook, not stand around looking coy!'

Leo propped himself against the sink and folded his arms. 'It shouldn't be for much longer. Now, I've invited all the Redmaynes to dinner next Thursday and I thought it might make it more informal, as well as stressing our status as a couple, if they came to my home instead of going out, and you did the cooking. You'd be able to pull out all the stops and really impress Bill with a five-star meal.'

'I could,' said Serena, wiping her hands on her apron, her professional interest roused in spite of herself. 'On the other hand, he's probably sick of going out to restaurants and eating elaborate meals. I gathered from what Oliver told me that his father's very traditional—he'd probably love a straightforward English, no-nonsense meal.'

'You may well be right.' Leo eyed her with something approaching respect. 'I'll leave it to you to decide what you give him.'

Serena busied herself emptying the contents of the blender into a bowl. 'Are you going to want me this weekend?' There was a tiny pause and she heard the ambiguity of her question hanging in the air. 'To act as your fiancée?' she added coldly.

'What else?' asked Leo with an ironic expression. 'There's a party tonight,' he told her when she only bit her lip, 'and a dinner tomorrow night. I was going on my own but Mary rang this morning to say that they'd heard the news and wanted me to bring you along, so you'd better be on your best behaviour. They're good friends of mine and won't be fooled by that silly performance you put on for Noelle. I won't need you on Sunday,' he added as an afterthought.

'Oh, thank you, sir!' cried Serena with exaggerated gratitude, but Leo only flicked her cheek, with a faint smile.

'I'll pick you up at half-past seven,' he said, and walked out.

Serena was surprised at how much she enjoyed the dinner party on Saturday night. Nick and Mary welcomed her so warmly that she felt horribly guilty at being there under false pretences. There were only four other guests, all other friends of Leo's, and they all accepted her as his fiancée without question. There were the inevitable congratulations to be got through, of course, but after that Serena relaxed and was able to join in the general laughter and conversation quite naturally.

Leo, too, was more relaxed than she had ever seen him. Sitting opposite him at table, she watched the way he threw back his head and laughed, and marvelled at the change from the ruthless banker she was more used to seeing. The characteristic coolness dissolved in the company of his friends, leaving him warmer and wittier and even more disturbingly attractive than usual.

She was very aware of him, of his smile and his laugh and his fingers around his glass. His hands kept catching her eye, evoking memories of them smoothing over her skin, and she would lose the thread of the conversation briefly before jerking her thoughts back to the dinner-table.

It was wonderful not to have to watch her tongue. The conversation was fast and sharp and Serena's natural astringency fitted in perfectly, provoking laughter instead of disapproving glances. She hadn't realised how wickedly funny Leo could be either; he and Nick made her laugh so much that she often had to wipe her eyes.

'Leo's been looking for a girl like you for a long time,' Mary told her, dragging her into the kitchen on the pretext of asking her advice about turning out the pudding. 'You're obviously perfect for each other.'

She was just as direct with Leo when they came to leave. 'I approve,' she said with a glance at Serena when he kissed her goodbye. 'She's just the girl for you.'

Serena didn't dare look at Leo as they walked out to the car, but he kept the conversation impersonal on the way back to her flat. She wondered, with a tightening knot of excitement, if he would kiss her again, but there was no one watching tonight and after he saw her to the door he merely wished her a brief goodnight and drove off, leaving Serena feeling curiously deflated.

The feeling lingered all Sunday. Normally, she loved having the whole day to herself, but that particular Sunday felt long and empty without him. It wasn't that she wanted to see him, she argued with herself; it was just that she had been so caught up in her new role that she was somehow getting used to him being there.

She tried distracting herself with the Sunday papers, but when the phone went she nearly knocked over her mug of coffee in her haste to get across the room, only to find her heart plummeting as she recognised her sister's voice instead of Leo's.

Well, why should he phone her?

Mastering her disappointment, Serena listened to Madeleine for half an hour, glad to hear that her sister sounded more positive. Everyone had been so kind, she said. Even her neighbour, whom she had only spoken to once or twice, had turned out to be a tower of strength. He was divorced too and one of his own children had been very ill once, so he knew what she was going through.

Serena listened and made the right noises. For now, Madeleine just needed to talk, she realised, and it left her free to wonder why on earth she had wanted it to be Leo on the phone. The only answer that suggested itself was so ridiculous that she dismissed it out of hand. She couldn't possibly just want to hear his voice.

She was glad to get back to work on Monday morning, deliberately planning complicated menus for the rest of the week to keep her so busy that she didn't have time to think. She didn't see Leo until the evening, when they had agreed to have a drink with Candace and Richard.

It wasn't nearly as bad as Serena had expected. Candace had got over the initial excitement of their sudden engagement and, frustrated by Leo and Serena's vague replies to her questions about wedding plans, she gave up eventually and let the talk move on to more general matters.

On Tuesday Leo took her to another reception and by the time Wednesday came round Serena was glad of a night off. She hadn't had any time to do any extra work in the kitchen this week and she wanted to do as much advance preparation as she could before the dinner on Thursday. She spent the afternoon getting as much as she could ready for Thursday's lunch, then turned her attention to the dinner.

She had decided on a deliciously light salmon mousse, followed by *boeuf en croute* and individual summer puddings. It wouldn't, she reflected wryly, win any marks for innovation, but she was banking on the fact that an arch-conservative like Bill Redmayne would probably prefer the freshest of ingredients beautifully cooked to any clever combinations of taste or artful presentation.

The summer puddings needed to be left overnight anyway. Serena made those first, then the salmon mousse.

As she worked, she thought about Leo. They had got on so much better since the dinner at Nick and Mary's and, as long as she didn't spend too much time thinking about how he had kissed her, she was able to talk to him quite naturally.

The trouble was that she *did* spend too much time thinking about it. She thought about it every time she noticed his mouth or his hands or the way he turned his head and smiled, and that made her wonder if he would kiss her again.

But if anything he was making an effort not to touch her. He took her home punctiliously, but never did more than wish her an impersonal goodnight. Serena didn't know whether to feel relieved or frustrated. It wasn't so much that she wanted him to kiss her, she reasoned; it was just that all the wondering whether he would or not was making her jumpy.

By the time she had finished the pastry, it was nearly nine o'clock and her feet were aching from standing all day. Even the workaholics had gone home, and the bank had a hushed, empty air. She sighed and stretched as she looked at her watch. She would just check that she had all her ingredients and equipment to take to Leo's tomorrow, then she would go home too.

She was adding a saucepan to the pile when the door behind her opened unexpectedly. Startled, Serena managed to hold on to the pan, but the lid fell to the floor with a clang which sounded even louder in the still quiet of the building.

Leo was standing in the doorway, looking as startled as she was. 'What are you doing here at this time of night?'

'I'm just getting things ready for tomorrow.' She bent to pick up the lid. She felt suddenly, stupidly shy.

'I didn't realise you'd have to work this late,' said Leo, frowning. He was wearing a very finely striped blue and white shirt, opened at the collar where he had loosened his tie, and his sleeves were rolled up to the elbow.

'I don't mind,' she said quickly, replacing the lid on the saucepan and setting it down with everything else that was to go tomorrow. 'Did. . .did you want something?'

'I just came down to make myself a sandwich. I've

been in meetings all day and didn't have time for lunch and now I'm starving, but I want to stay and finalise the draft proposal for Bill Redmayne.'

'I thought tomorrow was just going to be a social occasion?'

'It is, but if it goes well and Bill agrees to a meeting I want to be ready for him.' He suppressed a yawn and rubbed a hand over his face. There were lines of tiredness around his eyes and his hair was slightly rumpled as if he had been running his hands through it.

'You look tired,' sympathised Serena, and Leo sighed.

'Yes, I'll be glad when all this is over.' He glanced across at Serena. 'So will you.'

She twisted the diamond ring around her finger, watching the stones flash in the glare of the overhead spotlights. When the whole business of the merger was over, she would give Leo back his ring and walk out of his life. That was what she wanted, wasn't it?

Wasn't it?

'Yes,' she said flatly. 'I suppose so.' There was an awkward pause before she collected herself with an effort. 'I'll make you something to eat.'

'I may not be a very good cook, but I can make myself a sandwich,' Leo told her. 'You go home.'

'If you haven't eaten all day you need a proper meal,' said Serena stubbornly. She opened the fridge and studied the contents. Most of her ingredients were carefully calculated, but they wouldn't miss a couple of tomatoes and she could easily get some more eggs tomorrow. 'Do you like omelettes?'

'Yes, but you've been here quite long enough. I'm perfectly happy with a sandwich——'

'I'm making you an omelette,' she interrupted him firmly, lifting the omelette pan down from the rack.

'Think of it as me earning my salary if it makes you feel any better.'

'I think you've already done that,' said Leo unexpectedly. 'People keep coming up to me and congratulating me on my charming fiancée.'

'Charming?' Serena laughed. 'That doesn't sound like me!'

'Oh, I don't know,' said Leo, settling himself in a chair by the table. 'You can be quite captivating when you let those prickles down, and that fierce frankness of yours seems to be intriguing people rather than intimidating them. You're turning out to be even more of an asset than I thought. I certainly don't think anyone suspects that it's not a genuine engagement.'

Faint colour tinged Serena's cheeks. 'Even Noelle?'

'I think she thinks it's genuine, but she hasn't been quite as easy to distract as I'd hoped.' He rubbed his face tiredly again. 'Sometimes I get the impression she won't give up until we're married.'

'I hope you're not going to suggest we go that far!'

There was a tiny pause, then, 'Of course not,' said Leo. 'That *would* cost me, wouldn't it?'

Serena couldn't look at him. 'Perhaps tomorrow will convince her you're a lost cause,' she suggested.

'Let's hope so,' was all he said.

Turning in his chair so that he could lean back against the wall, he watched Serena as she moved around the kitchen. This was her domain, where the headstrong fieriness that so characterised her gave way to a calm competence and a sort of unhurried grace.

Unconscious of the interest in his gaze, Serena did what she did best, slicing tomatoes for a salad, cracking the eggs into a basin, chopping a selection of fresh herbs culled from the windowsill. The thick copper hair which had been tied back from her face so neatly at the beginning of the day was beginning to escape in wispy tendrils, and her expression reflected her absorption as she swirled butter in the pan, long lashes shadowing her cheeks.

The omelette was perfect, light and fluffy, and Leo ate it with relish while she ground some beans and made fresh coffee for them both.

'That was wonderful, thank you,' he said, pushing his empty plate aside at last with a smile that seemed to hit Serena in the solar plexus, and she dropped abruptly into the chair opposite, glad that it was there to break her fall. 'I feel ten times better for that,' he added, but she didn't think he looked that much better. Clasping both hands around his mug of coffee, he leant back against the wall and closed his eyes.

Serena let her eyes rest on his tired face and made an appalling discovery. She was in love with Leo Kerslake. Desperately, hopelessly in love with him.

I love you.

The words rang so loudly in her mind that for one ghastly moment she thought she had spoken them aloud. It felt as if they were booming round the room and bouncing off the walls, but Leo didn't move and she let her breath leak out slowly.

She couldn't possibly have done anything as silly as falling in love with Leo, could she? She didn't want to be in love with him. She didn't want to be in love with anybody. Hadn't Alex taught her how much hurt it could cause? Hadn't she watched her mother and Madeleine suffer, and determined that she would never do the same? Why, why, why hadn't she seen what was happening and done something about it before it was too late?

What could she have done? He hadn't tried to seduce her with sweet words or promises like Alex. Far from it. He had been arrogant and unpleasant and insulting, and she had fought the sharp tug of attraction for as long as she could. None of it had done any good. She loved him and she needed him. . .and she couldn't have him.

It wasn't as if Leo hadn't made his position crystal-clear. She wouldn't be the first girl to fall in love with him either, Serena realised dully. There must have been lots of other women in his life, and not one of them had been able to persuade him to give up his freedom. Why should she be any different? He might change his mind one day, perhaps, but if he did it wouldn't be for a bossy, belligerent cook! Her role was to preserve his freedom, not limit it, and she had better not forget it.

And there was no question of her telling him that she had had a change of heart, Serena realised sadly. Even if he didn't immediately leap to the conclusion that she was simply after his money—after all she had had to say about men and marriage—he would laugh in her face, and she wasn't prepared to risk her pride. Pride would be all that she had left when this was over.

Her heart cracked as she looked across the table. He was so close. She wanted to reach out and touch him, to smooth away the lines of tiredness from his face. If this had been their home, she could have got up and stood behind his chair to massage his neck. She could have leaned down and slipped her arms around him, kissed his ear, persuaded him upstairs to bed. . .

Leo opened his eyes so quickly that she didn't have time to look away, and for a long, long moment she stared into the silver depths before reality forced her gaze away. This wasn't a home, it was a bank, and whenever Leo went to bed it wouldn't be with her.

She cleared her throat. 'You should go home.'

Leo hesitated, looking at her as if the idea tempted him, then he shook his head. 'There's too much to do here,' he said.

'Is it so important to you, this merger?' she asked impulsively.

'Yes. Pushing this deal through is a test of my authority here at the bank. If it works, the board will have to finally accept that I'm in charge. I'm tired of having to watch my back, or waste valuable time negotiating with my own directors. If this goes through, I'll have the freedom to concentrate on the things that really matter.'

'It's your freedom that really matters to you, isn't it?' Serena said quietly.

Something flickered in the silver eyes. 'It's the same for you,' he reminded her. 'You're the only person I know who understands. You want the independence to do what you want as much as I do.'

Well, she had told him that. He wasn't to know that her much vaunted ambition to open a restaurant had crumbled to dust the moment she had looked across at him and acknowledged the truth knocking at her heart. All she wanted now was to be with him, to be able to reach out for him and know that he would never let her go. At a stroke the freedom and independence she had struggled for for so long had been transformed into loneliness and despair.

She got up suddenly and carried his plate to the sink. She couldn't bear to tell him the truth and see the horror and derision in his eyes. Much better that he should carry on believing that she was as committed to freedom as he was.

'Yes,' she said. 'I do understand. Of course I do.'

CHAPTER SEVEN

SOMEHOW Serena had imagined Leo living in a very modern flat or a smart town house, but the directions he gave her led to an elegant white house with a garden that swept down to the river.

'This is a very big house for a man who isn't interested in marriage and a family,' she said to him as he came out of the door to meet her. She had arranged to meet him there so that she could bring all her carefully packed ingredients and utensils in the van.

Leo shrugged as he helped her to carry everything into the kitchen. 'I inherited the house along with my shares when I came back. I could have sold it, I suppose, but I like the space. I hate feeling cramped, and the big reception-rooms are useful for entertaining.'

Marriage would cramp Leo as much as small rooms, Serena realised sadly. She felt light-headed with exhaustion. She had lain awake for most of the night, turning the immensity of her new discovery over and over in her mind and trying to convince herself that she was wrong, that the sharp clutch of desire had been no more than a temporary aberration brought on by tiredness.

The last thing she had wanted was to fall in love. She told herself that she would get over him, as she had got over Alex, but deep down she knew that what she felt for Leo was far deeper and stronger than her previous infatuation. Deeper, stronger and much, much more painful. She had to accept that she loved him, and that

there was absolutely nothing she could do about it—
apart from make sure that he never knew.

Inside, the rooms were light and well-proportioned,
each one beautifully decorated. Leo showed her the
sitting-room with its wide windows looking down to the
river, and opened a door into a long, elegant dining-
room. The polished mahogany table gleamed and the
rich, warm red walls were hung with oil-paintings.

But for Serena the best room was the kitchen. It was
huge, with big French windows opening on to the
garden. From the sink, she could see through another
window to the river which gleamed gold in the evening
sun. The units were hand-painted, the floor laid with
warm terracotta tiles and a vast pine table stood in the
middle of the floor, but somehow the room seemed
curiously empty, as if it had been staged for some glossy
magazine.

There were no cookery books, stuffed with yellowing
recipes cut out of newspapers and never used, no
shopping lists stuck to the fridge door, no mismatched
jars of herbs or faded tea-towels, no battered biscuit
tins, no embarrassing coffee-mugs that friends had
given years ago and refused to be broken. Everything
was put neatly away instead of being out, ready to be
used. There wasn't even a jar of coffee by the kettle.

'What a waste of a wonderful kitchen,' said Serena,
peering into the double ovens fixed to the wall.

'What's wrong with it?'

'There's nothing wrong with it. It just hasn't been
loved, that's all. A kitchen like this needs a cook,
someone to fill the cupboards with jams and chutneys
and sit at the table poring over recipes. It doesn't look
as if you've ever been in here.'

Leo looked around him, as if noticing the emptiness
for the first time. 'I rarely use the kitchen,' he admitted.
'I can just about open a tin, but I'd rather eat out. I

had the kitchen redone with the rest of the house, but I just let the designer do what she wanted.'

'It's such a waste,' mourned Serena again, running her hand lovingly along the edge of the table. 'I'd give anything for a kitchen like this.'

'Anything?' asked Leo, an odd note in his voice, and Serena glanced up to find him watching her with an unfathomable expression.

'Almost anything,' she said, and looked away. 'Well,' she went on with an assumption of briskness, 'I'd better get on. What time are they arriving?'

'Half-past seven. Do you want me to do anything?'

Take me in your arms. Tell me you love me. Ask me to share your life.

'No,' said Serena, tying her butcher's apron behind her. 'Just don't get in the way.'

Leo grinned, as if relieved at the return to her usual manner. 'I'll let you get on with it, then.'

Left alone, Serena swung automatically into action. The evening sun poured in through the side-window and filled the whole room with a golden glow as she prepared the vegetables, assembled the beef and whipped the cream for the summer puddings.

It really was a lovely kitchen, she thought wistfully. If it were hers, she would have copper-bottomed pans hanging from a rail and colourful pottery along the dresser above her cookery books. There would be a big bowl of fruit on the table and tempting-looking bottles of herb vinegars and olive oil and huge jars of mustard, and outside the glass doors fresh herbs would grow by the step.

She would sit at the table and plan menus and the room would always be full of sunshine and the warm, comforting aroma of baking, and about this time of the day the door would open and Leo would come in, smiling to find her in her favourite place. . .

The door opened, and Leo came in. Lost in her daydream, Serena smiled at him and there was a brief blaze of expression in his eyes before she remembered where she was and what she was supposed to be doing.

'You look very happy, Serena,' he commented.

She bent her head over the beef, now neatly wrapped in pastry, and adjusted one of the decorative leaves. 'I like cooking,' she muttered, horrified at how close she had come to revealing herself. She really must be more careful.

'You certainly look very comfortable in a kitchen,' said Leo, and she could hear the undercurrent of amusement rippling in his voice. Had he seen how she felt? 'I know you told me to keep out of your way, but I wondered if you wanted some time to change before they arrived.'

'I'll just lay the table, then everything's ready.'

Briskly practical once more, she set out the silver and the glasses on the dining-table, and placed a charmingly haphazard arrangement of flowers in the middle. Leo had told her that he would do the wine, and she could see three bottles of superlative red standing ready on the sideboard.

When she was ready at last, he took her upstairs. 'You may as well use my room,' he said, opening a door into a large, light room decorated in ivory and white. 'There's a bathroom through there——' he pointed at a connecting door '—and feel free to strew your things around. We may as well give the impression that you're in residence just in case Noelle gets nosy.'

Left alone, Serena couldn't help looking around her curiously. It was a cool, uncluttered room—rather like Leo himself—the room of a man without ties. Evidently he'd meant what he'd said when he'd declared that he would walk out on his life here at any time. There were no photographs, no hints of anyone who might have a claim to keep him here.

Serena had tortured herself wondering if his ruthless lack of commitment stemmed from a secret bitterness. Had he been in love, and disappointed? Had he offered up his freedom only to have it rejected, as she had been prepared to do for Alex? Like her, he might have been determined never to put himself in that position again.

Or he might simply like the freedom of knowing that he could move on whenever and wherever he wanted, Serena reminded herself. Either way, there were no clues to the private Leo here.

Her eyes fell on the wide bed. That would be the only place to discover the private Leo, she thought, and a wave of heat swept up from her toes at the idea.

The sun striped the bedcover invitingly and she felt a sudden, irresistible urge to climb on to the bed and lie back against the soft pillows. She glanced at her watch. Six o'clock. Plenty of time to get ready and she would be able to cope so much better this evening if she had a rest now. Surely twenty minutes couldn't do any harm? She wouldn't sleep, she would just put her feet up. . .

Her jeans were distinctly floury so she took them off and sat down on the edge of the bed, still half decided, but the pillows looked so tempting that she succumbed and leant back with a sigh, stretching out her long bare legs luxuriously. It was bliss to take the weight off her feet. Twenty minutes would do her the world of good.

The sun dazzled her eyes and she threw an arm across her face to shield them. It was such a comfortable bed. She wondered what it would be like to sleep in a cool, wide bed like this every night. What would it be like to reach out and find Leo there, with his lean, hard body and the crease in his cheek deepening as he bent down to kiss her and smiled? To be able to love him without reserve and fall asleep in his arms, knowing that when she woke he would still be there?

Serena's mind drifted, imagining, and the next thing she knew there was a warm finger stroking the soft skin on her inner arm. Still tangled in sleep, she stirred and smiled sleepily, letting her arm drop from her forehead.

'Serena?' The hand slid up her arm to her shoulder, then brushed a few wisps of hair away from her face with a feather-light touch. 'Serena, wake up.'

Very slowly, the long lashes lifted to reveal eyes that were green and soft and still dazed with dreams. 'Leo?' she murmured. This was a dream, wasn't it? Waking up to the smile in those silver eyes? 'Hello,' she said, and smiled dreamily again.

Leo drew in his breath sharply. 'I think you'd better wake up, Serena,' he said with a twisted smile. 'Or I won't answer for the consequences!'

She frowned as consciousness filtered back. She felt horribly disorientated. What was she doing lying here, staring up at Leo as if it were the most normal thing in the world to wake and find him there? Struggling upright, she rubbed her eyes with the heels of her hands like a child. 'What happened?'

'You've been asleep.' Leo got up from the bed where he had been sitting leaning over her. He was wearing black trousers and a crisp white shirt with the cuffs unfastened, and his hair was still damp from the shower.

He was freshly shaved. Serena could smell the clean, faintly masculine tang of his cologne and was shaken by a fierce gust of desire. She wanted to lay her hands against his face and trace the strong features with her fingers. She wanted to kiss her way along his jaw and down his throat. She wanted to unbutton his shirt and explore the firmness of his body and feel his heart beating against her own.

'What time is it?' she asked in a high, tight voice as she struggled to control the wayward drift of her thoughts.

'Quarter to seven.'

'Quarter to *seven*?' She echoed, jerked abruptly back to the present. 'Why didn't you wake me sooner?'

'You were sleeping so soundly, I thought you must have been tired,' said Leo. 'When I put my head round the door, you were draped most invitingly across my bed, dead to the world, so I just carried on around you.'

'I didn't mean to fall asleep,' she said guiltily. 'I was just going to rest my feet for a while.'

'It doesn't matter,' he told her, amused. 'That's what beds are for. . .among other things.' His eyes dropped to the long, slender legs still stretched across the bed and he watched glintingly as Serena flushed scarlet and swung them to the floor, conscious for the first time that she was half-naked.

'I. . .I'd better have a shower,' she said, tugging down her T-shirt as far as it would go over her pants.

'Just help me with these cuff-links, will you? Then I'll leave you in peace.'

He dropped a pair of gold cuff-links into her palm and held out an arm. Serena's fingers felt stiff and unwieldy as she bent over his wrist, burningly aware of the intimacy of the scene and the scantiness of her clothing. One T-shirt and a skimpy pair of pants weren't much defence the hazy excitement of his nearness. Her hands shook as they brushed against his and she concentrated fiercely on the task as she tried to get her breathing under control.

His hands were perfectly steady. Strong, brown, infinitely competent, with clean square nails. They were just hands, Serena told herself desperately. There was absolutely no reason for her to quiver at the thought of them drifting over her skin. Leo had probably hardly noticed that she was standing so close to him with practically no clothes on, she thought bitterly as her fingers fumbled with the second cuff-link.

'There.' With a sigh of relief she stepped back, and made the mistake of looking up at him. He was smiling slightly, his silver-grey eyes warm. They seemed to reach deep into Serena, lighting an answering warmth deep inside her, and, hardly knowing what she was doing, she smiled back at him rather shakily.

'Serena——' Leo changed his mind abruptly about what he was going to say, and bit back the words with a visible effort. 'It's getting late,' he said instead. 'You'd better get ready.'

It was only a look, only a hint that he might like her more than he admitted, but Serena treasured the warmth inside her as she showered and changed. Leo had asked—told!—her to wear one of the dresses he had bought her. She had grumbled, of course, but if she was honest the black dress was her favourite. Absolutely plain, almost severe, it relied on a dramatically simple cut and the texture of the fabric for its stunning effect. The low neckline emphasised the creaminess of her skin and the matt black was in striking contrast to the glorious copper hair and the long, vivid green eyes.

Serena smoothed it down in front of the mirror. What would Leo think? He had seen the dress, of course, but tonight she had piled her hair up on to the top of her head and she eyed herself doubtfully. The formal style drew attention to the pure sweep of her throat and shoulders and the proud tilt of her head, but she thought the effect was rather spoilt by the soft tendrils escaping around her face. She felt very self-conscious in make-up, too, but somehow the dress demanded it. Serena hardly recognised herself with that sultry-looking red mouth.

If she had had more time she might have been tempted to wipe it all off, but there were things to do in the kitchen. Giving herself a careless spray of perfume, she hurried downstairs.

In his typically high-handed way, Leo had announced that he had found a girl to help her in the kitchen. Serena had protested indignantly that she didn't need any help, but he had been adamant. Jill was to do the clearing up and keep an eye on things in the kitchen so that Serena could spend as much time as possible with their guests. Normally Serena hated delegating any part of the preparation, but Jill was so obviously sensible that she was able to give her last-minute instructions with an easy mind and go in search of Leo.

He was in the sitting-room, standing by the window and looking out to the river, hands thrust impatiently into the pockets of his dark trousers. The austerely black dinner-jacket suited him and made his eyes look even more silver and striking than ever in his dark face. He looked devastatingly attractive as he turned at her entrance and Serena was glad that she had the door-handle to hang on to as the breath leaked out of her and her bones dissolved with longing.

For a long moment they stared at each other across the room, and then he took his hands out of his pockets. 'Is everything ready?'

She nodded, not trusting herself to speak.

'Come over here,' he said when she continued to cling dumbly to the door. 'I've got something for you.' He drew a flat package out of the inside pocket of his jacket.

'What is it?' Serena walked over half reluctantly to join him in front of the mantelpiece. She stared down at the leather box he handed her.

'Open it.'

Moistening her lips, she lifted the lid. Inside lay an exquisite diamond necklace flanked by a pair of matching earrings. The stones sparkled against the red velvet lining, glitteringly beautiful. Serena swallowed, opened her mouth and then shut it. She simply couldn't think of anything to say. She lifted her eyes to look wordlessly at Leo.

'Aren't you going to put them on?'

'I can't wear these.' She found her voice at last. 'They're far too valuable.'

'Rubbish,' said Leo as if he was making an effort to sound harsh. 'They're props, like the ring. With any luck they'll remind Oliver Redmayne that you're my fiancée, not his,' he added with a sardonic look. 'Go on, put them on.'

Serena's hands were unsteady as she took out her gold knot earrings and fixed the diamonds in their place. They were window-dressing for this ghastly charade they were playing, a parody of a gift of love. They're props, they're props, they're props, she chanted to herself.

Leo eyed the earrings critically like a connoisseur. 'Very nice,' he said finally, lifting the necklace from its velvet bed. The diamonds winked and glittered between his fingers. 'Turn round.'

Serena turned obediently to face the antique mirror above the mantelpiece, agonisingly conscious of his hands settling the necklace against her skin, brushing the nape of her neck as he fastened the clasp. She touched the stones nervously, shifting them against her cleavage, and Leo clicked his tongue in exasperation.

'Don't fiddle with it!' He readjusted the necklace with warm fingers, then rested his hands on her shoulders. 'There. . .what do you think?'

He was standing behind her, talking to her reflection

in the mirror. The diamonds glinted and blurred in front of her eyes and she blinked the sudden sting of tears away. There was no point in wishing this was for real. Wishing wouldn't change things. 'They're beautiful,' she said huskily.

'So are you. . .' Leo's hands slid down her bare arms to slide around her waist and draw her back against him. Bending his head, he dropped a kiss on her shoulder.

She nearly gasped at the electrifying desire that jolted through her as his lips touched her skin. 'We. . .we don't need to pretend when we're alone,' she managed at last.

Leo lifted his head briefly to meet her gaze in the mirror—her eyes were dark and wide and torn with longing. 'No, we don't, do we?' he said deliberately, and lowered his mouth once more to burn a trail of warm, tantalising kisses along her shoulder and up the soft, pure line of her throat. Instinctively, Serena closed her eyes against the spine-clenching grip of desire and a murmur of helpless pleasure escaped her.

'Beautiful,' Leo whispered raggedly against her ear.

Serena's resistance crumbled and she gave in and leant back against the unyielding strength of his body, powerless before the heart-stopping exploration of his lips, so warm and wickedly exciting against her throat. Her fingers clutched at the sleeves of his jacket and his arms tightened around her in response, gathering her closer.

His mouth continued its slow, deliberate, devastating onslaught, drifting to the nape of her neck and then up the other side of her neck in a trail of fire and delight that left Serena weak-kneed and quivering with desire.

When the doorbell rang neither of them reacted immediately. Leo's mouth stilled reluctantly against her skin, and Serena lifted her lashes to find herself looking at her own and Leo's reflection in the mirror. Leo's dark head was buried against her hair and she was leaning back against him, her throat arched invitingly and her mouth curved into a languorous smile that faded slowly as Leo raised his head and they stared into each other's reflected eyes.

The doorbell clamoured again. Leo's hands slid back up her arms to her shoulders and he set her upright again with a wry smile. 'I think our guests have arrived in the nick of time.'

Bill Redmayne was a big, choleric-looking man with ferocious eyebrows and gimlet eyes. He favoured Serena with a suspicious stare as she moved forward to greet him, and she wondered if she looked as distracted as she felt. Her blood was pounding beneath her skin and her legs were so weak that she was half afraid she would simply dissolve into a puddle of frustrated desire on the floor.

Oliver greeted her with a warm smile and a kiss on the cheek, but she was still so dazed from the feel of Leo's arms about her that she hardly noticed and only smiled absently in reply to Noelle's distinctly cool greeting.

The evening passed in a blur. Serena felt oddly distanced from it all. She talked and smiled and fended off Oliver's attempts at flirtation, but it was as if she was watching it all on film and the only reality was Leo's dark presence at the other end of the table.

She strummed with the memory of his touch. Leo was being the perfect host but she knew that he was as aware of her as she was of him. Even though they were careful not to look at each other, Serena was so attuned to him that she knew every time he smiled, every time he turned his head.

The meal was perfect, the salmon mousse delicate and flavourful, the beef cooked to just the right pinkness, the vegetables crisp and fresh. When Serena brought the summer puddings in, Bill Redmayne went so far as to rub his hands together.

'My favourite,' he told her gruffly, picking up his spoon. 'I can't stand these fancy puddings they give you nowadays. It makes a nice change to have some decent food without everything swimming around in some bloody coulis or whatever they call it, I can tell you. Oliver wants to open a restaurant serving that sort of muck, but I've told him it won't work.'

'A country club, not a restaurant, Father,' Oliver corrected him wearily. It was obviously an old argument.

'Whatever you want to call it, if you've got any sense you'll take some advice from Serena here about serving food. She obviously knows what she's about.'

'Perhaps you should take Serena on board as a consultant, Oliver,' Noelle suggested sweetly, and he grinned.

'That's a great idea. What about it, Serena?'

Serena's eyes flickered to Leo. He was refilling Noelle's glass, but he glanced up and their eyes met briefly through the candlelight. 'I've got rather a lot on my plate at the moment,' she apologised.

Bill gave a crack of laughter. 'Spoken like a sensible woman! You're much better off sticking with Leo here than getting involved in my son's mad schemes.'

In spite of Serena's preoccupation, she had recognised a kindred spirit in Bill Redmayne. The fearsome image hid a sharp sense of humour and a brusque kindness that she imagined few people, including his own children, guessed at.

Noelle and Oliver watched in amazement as their tyrannical father unbent in her company, and they kept exchanging wondering looks across the table. It was left to Leo to entertain them, while Serena charmed Bill with a complete lack of affectation. Later, she couldn't remember anything she'd said to him, but decided it was her own obsession with Leo that had enabled her to talk to him without any of the reserve she would have felt if she had been trying to impress him. Whatever it was, Bill was quite won over.

Serena thought they would never go. Jill had cleared up the kitchen and gone by the time she went along to make the third pot of coffee. The merger hadn't been mentioned once. She even began to wonder if Bill had forgotten why they were there, but when they finally left he turned to Leo at the front door and poked a stubby finger at his chest.

'I didn't like the idea of this merger when it first came up, I have to admit. I've heard you're a cool operator, but a risk-taker, and I don't want Redmayne and Co gambled away. Still, you're obviously sensible enough to find yourself a good wife, so you can get your secretary to ring mine and fix up a meeting for next week. I'm not promising anything, mind.' He held up a warning finger as Oliver and Noelle exchanged jubilant looks. 'But I'll listen to what you've got to say and then I might—*might*!—consider your proposal.'

At last they were gone. Serena and Leo watched the lights of the car disappear down the road before they turned to walk back into the house in a silence charged with electric tension.

Now that she was alone with him, Serena was suddenly terribly nervous. She practically ran into the kitchen to retrieve her apron, wrapping it round her as if it was her last defence. Back in the sitting-room, she began gathering up the coffee-cups, rattling them in their saucers as she put them on the tray. 'I think that went quite well, don't you?' she said brightly, unable to look at him.

'Thanks to you,' said Leo, watching the coppery head

bent determinedly over the tray. 'You had that old tyrant eating out of your hand and the meal was a stroke of genius. If he agrees to the merger, it'll be because of that summer pudding!'

'Oh, I don't know. . . I'm sure he'll be convinced by your proposal, and when he realises how keen Noelle and Oliver are. . .' Serena realised that she was gabbling, and decided to concentrate on breathing instead.

She was still holding a cup and saucer as Leo walked over to her. 'No,' he said, taking them from her and setting them back down on the table. 'If he agrees, it'll be thanks to you.' Bending his head, he kissed first one corner of her mouth and then the other. 'Thank you,' he murmured softly.

'I'm glad you feel you're getting your money's worth,' said Serena with enormous difficulty. Her breath kept getting stuck in her throat and she couldn't tear her eyes from his mouth.

'I think I got more than I bargained for,' Leo told her slowly, looking down into her face, his expression suddenly intent. 'Much more.'

'I'll just wash up these cups. . .' Serena began to back away, terrified by the strength of the feelings that threatened to overwhelm her.

'Leave them. Jill's going to come in again in the morning to finish off anything that's left.'

'It's no trouble. . .' she began, then her voice died as he reached out and drew her towards him. 'I don't think this is a very good idea,' she managed, stepping breathlessly back out of his grasp.

Leo only smiled. 'Don't you? I do. I've been thinking about it all evening, and so have you. Now take off that bloody apron and come here!'

Her heart thumped and thudded against her ribs as she looked helplessly back at him, snarled in a terrible web of need and desire. Could she really sacrifice her pride like this? Hadn't she decided to hang on to that if nothing else? But pride, it seemed, had dissolved along with everything else that had once been so important to her. Her fierce independence, her ambitions and now her famously stubborn pride had crumbled one by one in the face of her growing need for Leo. He was all that mattered.

He was waiting for her, making no move to persuade her, the silver smile glimmering still in his eyes. She felt as if she was teetering at the edge of an abyss. One step was all it would take, and there would be no going back.

Slowly, very slowly, she untied her apron and lifted the tape over her head. Dropping it on a chair, she looked back at him with eyes that were dark and vulnerable with temptation.

'Come here,' he said again, softly, smiling.

Serena drew an unsteady breath, hesitated once more, then went.

CHAPTER EIGHT

LEO lifted his hands to hold her face tenderly, tracing the deceptively fragile cheekbones with his thumbs. 'Don't look like that, Serena,' he said gently, misunderstanding her hesitation. 'You're not committing yourself forever. Neither of us expects any promises about the future. Let's just have tonight.'

No commitment, no promises. No future, no forever. It wasn't what Serena wanted to hear but, as she looked up into Leo's face, she knew that even if tonight was all she ever had it would be enough.

'Let's have tonight,' she echoed softly.

He took her hand and led her without speaking up to his bedroom, up to the big, wide bed where she had dreamt of him only hours ago. She took off her shoes, watching as he switched on the bedside lamp, and then turned to draw her from the shadows into its soft yellow glow. Wordlessly, he removed her earrings and placed them very carefully on the table by the bed.

Serena felt suspended, adrift in a sea of sensation. She couldn't feel the carpet beneath her bare feet. All she could feel was the strumming anticipation and Leo's deft, unhurried fingers against the nape of her neck as he unfastened the necklace. The diamonds shimmered in the light as he laid them down by the earrings.

Still without speaking, without taking his eyes from her face, he found the zip at the back of her dress and undid it very slowly until he could slide it from her shoulders to fall in a puddle of material at her feet. His gaze followed the dress and then travelled hungrily back up her body, which was luminous in the soft light, and Serena felt her heart slam at his expression. He might not want her forever but for tonight he was hers, and at that realisation the last of her doubts and hesitations disappeared.

Leo spread his hands around her waist and drew her against him. She smiled up at him, surprising such a blazing look in his eyes that her smile faltered for a moment, but the warm possession of his hands against her skin reassured her and she leant at last to kiss the angle of his jaw and throat, the angle that had been haunting her dreams long before she would admit it. She saw him smile, felt him smile against her lips as she drifted kisses across his cheek to his mouth.

'Serena. . .' He muttered her name between long, breathless kisses, pulling her hair free of its combs and burying his face in the silky tumble of copper.

Her fingers were less steady than his, but she managed to undo his bow-tie and let it drop to the floor beside her dress before fumbling at the buttons of his shirt. He had to help her in the end, but at last she was able to tug his shirt free and put her arms around him, gasping at the shivery shock of skin on skin.

Their mouths found each other in kisses that grew deeper and more demanding as the slow, exquisite burn of desire that had held them silent up to now flamed higher and higher until it consumed the quiet room in its blaze, leaving only taste and touch and the insistent beat of their hearts.

As the flame grew, so their hands explored each other hungrily, almost frantically, pulling off the last of the clothes between them. Laughing shakily at their sudden desperation, they sank down on to the bed, down into a chasm of swinging sensation.

Half afraid of the feelings spinning her out of control, Serena clung to Leo as his lips and his hands traced burning patterns of need on her skin, treasuring each slender curve of her body, each enticing hollow. She dug her fingers into the hard muscles of his shoulder, giddy with the feel of his sleek, strong body possessing hers with such mastery, and then, as he moved over her and smiled down into her face, she forgot to be afraid. Abandoning herself to wave after crashing wave of pleasure, she let him take her on and up to where there was nothing but timeless, explosive joy and the knowledge that they belonged to each other utterly.

Aeons later, when Serena opened her eyes, the first thing she saw was the glimmer of the diamond ring on her hand where it clutched still at his shoulder. Leo's face was buried against her throat and she could hear his breathing slowly returning to normal. Loving the weight of his body on her, she relaxed the grip of her fingers and kissed his ear, which was the only bit of him she could reach with her lips.

She felt him smile against her throat. 'Do you still think it wasn't a good idea?' he teased, raising his head to smooth the hair away from her face. In the warm glow of the bedside lamp, his face held an expression of tenderness that Serena had never expected to see.

'We-ell. . .' Serena pretended to consider, twisting her foot so that she could run her instep seductively over the rough hairs on the back of his calves. 'I suppose it was better than washing up!'

Leo laughed, but his smile faded as he propped himself on one elbow and ran one finger down her throat to circle one breast. 'Still fighting the passion inside you, Serena?'

Her eyes had darkened at the caress of his hand, so strong, so sure, so exciting against her breast. 'No,' she whispered, and reached up to pull his head back down to hers. 'Not any more.'

* * *

Serena stirred and stretched, opening her eyes slowly to see Leo sitting on the edge of the bed beside her, stroking her arm. He was half dressed, his shirt-sleeves rolled up and a blue tie slung untied round his neck.

'I've brought you a cup of tea,' he said, setting a cup down on the bedside table.

Serena pulled herself up against the pillows, taking the duvet with her to cover her nakedness. 'Thank you.' After the passion of the previous night she felt absurdly shy in the bright morning light, but when she glanced at him under her lashes she saw that his eyes were warm and smiling, and she felt her insides knot with renewed desire as she relaxed back into the pillows and smiled back.

Something flared in Leo's eyes and he leant forward to kiss her, a gentle kiss warm with the memories of all they had shared last night. Careless of the fact that she had just woken up, she put her arms around his neck and kissed him back until he pulled away reluctantly.

'I've got to go,' he said with regret. 'I've got a breakfast meeting in the City at half-past seven.'

'Not with Noelle?' asked Serena, but it must have been obvious to Leo that she knew perfectly well that she had no reason to feel jealous, for he grinned.

'No, *not* with Noelle.' He twisted a strand of her shining hair around his finger. 'I should have left you to sleep, but I didn't want to go without saying goodbye.'

She touched his hair, her eyes very green and direct. 'I'm glad you did, but I wish you could stay.'

'Don't tempt me, Serena!' he said, catching her against him for one hard, possessive kiss before he stood up abruptly. 'I must go. Will you be at the bank later?'

'Of course,' she smiled, and he rested his hand briefly against her cheek.

'I'll see you there, then.'

When he had gone, Serena stretched luxuriously, hardly noticing the rapidly cooling tea as she remembered last night. Their lovemaking had been so glorious, so fulfilling, that it was impossible to believe that it hadn't meant anything to Leo.

Sternly, she tried to remind herself of his determination never to commit himself to anyone, but this morning, with the early morning sun falling across the bed and her body strumming with contentment, she couldn't stop her heart singing with hope whenever she thought about the expression in his eyes as he had kissed her.

Incandescent with happiness, she hummed as she drove home to change. Never had she seen London looking so colourful. The trees were decked out in May green, brightly coloured window-boxes were unfurling in the sun and every door seemed to be freshly painted. Even the traffic lights seemed expressly designed to add to the kaleidoscope of colour.

Memories of the joy Leo had shown her insulated her with happiness and optimism for the future. She had had a change of heart about marriage once she had learnt what love could be; what was to stop Leo doing the same?

She smiled at a shopkeeper pulling down a striped canopy in readiness for another sunny day. She felt as if nothing could touch her, as if nothing could mar the sparkling promise of the day.

She was wrong.

Back at her flat, she jumped quickly into the shower and then wandered out into the sitting-room to listen to any messages on her answering machine while she rubbed at her damp hair with a towel, but her happiness vanished at the sound of Madeleine's broken voice asking her to ring back as soon as she could.

Her hand shook as she dialled the number Madeleine

had left on the machine. It would be the early hours of the morning in Florida, but Madeleine had sounded desperate. As she had guessed, her sister answered the phone so quickly that she must have been sitting right beside it.

'I'm in the hospital,' she said, sounding so weary that Serena wanted to cry. How could she have been so happy when Madeleine was in such distress? 'Bobby got suddenly worse, so I used that money you sent to make sure he came to the best place. Now the doctors say they really need to operate, but it's going to be so expensive. I don't think I've got enough left, and Bobby's so sick. . .'

She broke down in tears and Serena took a deep breath, struggling to keep her voice calm and reassuring as she coaxed the details out of her sister.

'I think I know where I can get hold of some more money,' she said at last. She felt a little sick at the idea of asking Leo for money, today of all days, but she had no choice. She couldn't leave a small boy fighting for his life because she didn't want to remind Leo that their relationship was essentially a business one. 'Try not to worry, Madeleine. The important thing is for Bobby to have the operation as soon as possible. I. . .I'll get some money to you somehow. Tell the doctors you'll have enough to pay for the operation by the end of the day.'

Madeleine was almost incoherent with gratitude. 'I feel terrible,' she sobbed. 'You've sent so much already and I only ever seem to ring you to ask for something, but I don't know who else to turn to.'

'That's what families are for,' said Serena firmly.

'But you can't afford it. . .where's all this money coming from?'

Serena smiled wryly into the receiver. 'It's a long

story,' she said. 'I'll tell you all about it one day but, for now, Bobby is all that matters.'

Leo came to the door of his office when Lindy buzzed him to say that Serena wanted a word with him, but his welcoming smile faded as he saw her expression.

'Serena! I didn't think you'd be in until later.'

'I need to talk to you,' she said. Her throat felt bone-dry. 'It's rather important. Have you got a few minutes?'

'Of course.' He held the door wide for her. 'Hold all my calls, will you, Lindy?'

Serena stood by the window, fiddling nervously with the diamond ring and wondering where to begin.

Leo came to stand beside her but she couldn't look at him, afraid that if she did she would throw herself on his chest and burst into tears. She had borne the responsibility for her mother and Madeleine for so long now that she no longer knew how to beg for help.

'You don't look like the same girl I left this morning,' he said eventually. 'What is it?'

There seemed no easy way to explain. Perhaps it would be best just to tell him the truth. 'I need some money,' she told him baldly.

There was a frozen pause. 'What?' said Leo, danger-ously quiet, and she swallowed.

'I. . .I wondered if I could have an advance on the money we agreed.'

He stepped deliberately away from her. 'The merger hasn't gone through yet,' he reminded her tonelessly.

'I know, but it's been a week, and I thought——'

'You thought that since you'd gone to the lengths of sleeping with me you deserved a little extra?'

'No!' cried Serena, flinching at his tone. 'It's not like that!'

'Isn't it? I've got to hand it to you, Serena, you're

pretty cool. Most girls would have had the decency to wait a few days before expecting some demonstration of appreciation, but not you. The bed's still warm and you're already demanding money for services rendered! You were good, but not that good!'

Serena felt very cold. 'You don't understand.'

'Oh, I understand only too well,' he said savagely, turning away from her in disgust. 'You've never made any secret of how much money means to you, but you nearly had me fooled last night. I didn't realise until now quite how clever you are. You set me up like a fool and now you have the nerve to come here demanding to be paid! And to think I thought that cooking was your profession!'

'How dare you?' said Serena, white-faced. 'It wasn't like that last night and you know it!'

'Do I? It certainly looks like that from where I'm standing.'

She drew a shaky breath. This was far, far worse than she had feared. Did last night count for nothing with him? 'You don't understand,' she tried again shakily. 'If you'd only let me explain——'

'I don't want to listen to any explanations!' he said bitterly.

'Leo, *please*. . .'

'I said I don't want to hear,' he bit out between clenched teeth. 'You're just like all the rest. Last night you said you wanted me but I should have known that all you really wanted was my money.'

'Yes, you should!' Bitter anger ripped through her numb sense of shock. 'Why are you so surprised when you *bought* me? You knew that money was the only reason I agreed to your stupid charade in the first place. Or did you think I really wanted to deceive my friends by pretending to be your fiancée? Do you really think I've enjoyed being treated like some plastic dummy to be dressed up and discarded when you've finished with me? Of course I want to be paid for it! I've earned it— or do I have to sleep with you a few more times before you think you've had value for money?' she added deliberately.

'You've already demanded a more than generous advance,' said Leo flatly. He was very white about the mouth and a muscle hammered in his cheek. 'The agreement was for you to be paid when the merger went through.'

Serena couldn't believe they were talking so bitterly about money and agreements and mergers after the hours of sweetness they had shared such a short time ago. 'I need some now,' she said doggedly.

'Why?'

It was too late for him to ask that now, she thought furiously. If he had asked right at the start she would have told him, but instead he was so blinkered by his own stupid prejudices that he wasn't even prepared to listen to what she had to say. If he had cared about her at all, he would have trusted her enough to know that only the most pressing of reasons would have made her ask for money. He wouldn't have needed to ask her why.

As it was, he could dismiss everything he knew about her because it was so much easier to believe she fitted into some narrow category that he recognised. No, he didn't care about her. He had probably only made love to her last night because she had been available and she had fallen into his arms.

Her only comfort was that she hadn't told him how much she loved him. If he was too stupid and narrow-minded to see it for himself, she certainly wasn't going to tell him. Nor was she going to share Madeleine's misery with a man who could even think she would sleep with him for anything less than love.

'That's none of your business,' she said, clenching her jaw to stop it trembling. She *wouldn't* cry in front of him!

'Acquired a taste for diamonds and expensive clothes, have you?' sneered Leo. 'You certainly took to them like a natural.'

'Are you going to give me some money or not?' she asked stonily.

'What happens if I don't?'

Serena thought of Bobby lying in his hospital bed, of the tears in Madeleine's voice. She *had* to send some money today. 'I'll tell everyone that our engagement is a mockery,' she said evenly.

'I see you add blackmail to your other talents!'

'I'm not asking you for anything more than we agreed.' Serena could feel her voice breaking, and drew a steadying breath. 'I've done my part. Noelle thinks we're engaged, and Bill Redmayne has agreed to a meeting. All I want is an advance on the money you'll be giving me anyway in a few weeks if the merger goes through.' She hesitated. 'You said last night that you were grateful.'

'I said I lot of things last night I didn't mean.' Leo strode over to his desk and pulled out a cheque-book. 'This should be interesting! How much do you think one night with you is worth, Serena?'

Her nails were digging into her palms. She had no idea how much Bobby's operation would be, but she had an idea that medical costs were horrendously expensive without insurance. 'Five thousand pounds,' she said, astonished at the coolness of her own voice, and Leo's dark head jerked up.

'You were good, but you weren't that good!' he said again contemptuously. 'No woman's worth that much for a roll in the dark.'

A roll in the dark? Was that really all it had been for

him? Serena felt as if vicious claws were tearing at her heart. 'Do you really think I'd sleep with you for less?' she retorted, wanting only to hurt him as much as he'd hurt her.

For a moment she thought Leo was going to reach across the desk and grab her by the throat and she took an involuntary step backwards before he lowered his head and scribbled out the cheque. Tearing it out of the book, he came round the desk and tucked it with deliberate contempt down her cleavage. 'There you are,' he said. 'This is an advance, not a bonus. Given that sex wasn't included in our original agreement, it seems as if I'm the one who had the bonus, doesn't it?'

Every word struck Serena like a stone. She took the cheque from the front of her shirt and folded it with shaking hands before putting it in her pocket. 'Think of it as a bonus if it makes you feel any better,' she said, her tone as biting as his. 'You certainly won't be getting another one. I don't want you to touch me again.'

There was a pause. Leo put his face close to hers. 'I wouldn't want to,' he said very distinctly. 'I'm not enjoying this charade any more than you are, Serena, and I'm doing everything I can to make sure we can finish it as soon as possible, because the sooner that happens the sooner I never have to see you again.

'Until then, we abide by the agreement you're being paid so much for. I'll try and excuse you from as many invitations as possible, but when you do have to be on show you're going to carry on as before. If anyone so much as suspects that this conversation has taken place, you can give me that five thousand pounds back. Is that understood?'

'Yes.' Her heart was cracking, tearing apart. She was desperate to get out of the room before she cried out with the pain.

'In that case you can start by walking out of that door

smiling, so that Lindy has no idea that we're not the
romantic couple she sincerely believes us to be.'

Without another word, Serena turned and walked
out. She never knew how she did it, but somehow she
managed to smile at Lindy and keep the same fixed grin
on her face all the way down to the kitchen. It was a
wonderful relief to close the door behind her and lean
back against it, squeezing her eyes shut to try and stop
the tears.

After a while, she went over to the table, moving
stiffly like an old woman, and slumped down on one of
the chairs, burying her head in her arms. How was it
possible to love someone so much and hate them at the
same time? She had been so happy when she'd woken
up that morning, so confident that Leo felt the same.
She kept seeing his smile as he had leant forward to
kiss her, overlaid, as if in a nightmare, by the icy
contempt in his eyes when she had asked him for
money.

Why couldn't he have listened?

She gave a shuddering sigh and leant back in the
chair, wiping the tears from her cheeks with her palms.
Would it have been so difficult for him to give her the
benefit of the doubt, to wonder why she had agreed to
act as his fiancée in the first place? A man who loved
her would have wanted to help her without needing to
know the reasons. A man who loved her would have
taken her in his arms and comforted her. He would
have remembered the night before and known that she
loved him too.

But Leo didn't love her.

Serena's blood ran cold whenever she thought of how
near she had come to telling him how much she loved
him. That would have been the ultimate humiliation—
not that he would have believed her. She had been a
fool to think for a minute that falling in love with him

could end in anything other than misery. Hadn't she learnt her lesson from Alex? Leo was just the same. A few kisses, a few smiles, and they thought that women would fall into their arms.

As she had.

She was furious with herself, even angrier with Leo. He had used her and insulted her and she was damned if she was going to let him know how much he had hurt her. Taking the cheque from her pocket, she put it in her bag and went straight to the bank with her head held high.

Over the next three weeks, she deliberately kept her anger at boiling-point. It was the only way she knew to forget how much she still loved him. The knowledge still lurked like a raw wound deep inside her, but at least the hot rush of fury whenever she remembered the things he had said to her helped dull the pain.

He sent down a curt note informing her that he didn't want to see her that weekend and that he would tell everyone that she had flu. That suited Serena. She stayed in her flat and made huge quantities of soup for the freezer, which was the only therapy she knew. She forced herself to sound cheerful when she talked to Madeleine on the phone, but she spent most of the weekend furiously stirring huge pots of simmering vegetables while the tears poured down her face.

Hearing nothing more from Leo, she went into work as usual on Monday, but he didn't come to lunch. She didn't see him until Wednesday afternoon, when he walked into the kitchen without warning. She was scrubbing saucepans and wishing she could rub away the memories as easily.

At the sound of the door she glanced over her shoulder and her heart jumped to her throat. She gave no sign of it, though, turning ostentatiously back to the pots and only acknowledging his presence by scrubbing harder.

'Bill Redmayne and I had a meeting this morning,' said Leo, closing the door behind him. He looked taut with strain. 'And he's agreed to think about my proposals for the merger.'

'I hope you're not expecting me to cheer,' snapped Serena, slamming a saucepan on to the draining-board to cover the gust of desire to go and put her arms around him.

'This concerns you, so you might as well listen,' he said icily.

'Short of throwing you out of my kitchen, it doesn't look as if I've got much choice, does it?'

'I hate to remind you, Serena, but this is in fact *my* kitchen.'

Serena submerged another pot and picked up the scourer once more. 'Why don't you just get to the point?'

'Very well.' Leo cast her a cold glance. 'Bill's going to think about the possibility of a merger and let me have his decision in three weeks' time.'

'So we only have to put up with each other for another three weeks?'

'Exactly. Unfortunately, he's decided he wants another good look at me before he finally makes up his mind. He's invited us both up to his house in Yorkshire for that weekend, and he particularly wants you to be there.' Leo's tone made it clear that he didn't share Bill's enthusiasm for her company. 'I've accepted for both of us. It'll be your final appearance as my fiancée. Whatever Bill decides, we can go our separate ways after that. We'll just say we changed our minds about getting married after all.'

Serena's hands stilled. 'So that will be the end?'

There was a tiny pause, then Leo turned for the

door. 'That'll be the end,' he agreed, and went out without another word.

Serena didn't know whether she longed for the weekend in Yorkshire to be over, or dreaded its arrival. When it was over, she would never see Leo again. She had handed in her notice at the bank, where Personnel had received it without surprise, assuming that she was leaving to marry Leo. She didn't know if she could bear the thought of not seeing him, and yet the weeks that followed were torture.

Once or twice a week she would put on one of the smart outfits Leo had bought her and go with him to a drinks party or a dinner or the theatre, where she would smile and smile and wonder that no one seemed to notice that her heart was breaking. Certainly no one guessed that she and Leo barely said a word to each other except in public. He was coldly formal, not even bothering to disguise his contempt, and Serena in turn retreated behind an icy mask.

They were both very careful not to touch each other if they could avoid it, but sometimes in public Leo would take her arm or rest his hand against the small of her back in a gesture of intimacy that clutched at Serena's heart so viciously that she would flinch. She longed to turn and burrow into him for comfort, to tell him about Bobby and feel his arms close about her, but then his hand would drop as if he couldn't bear to touch her any longer.

On most occasions they didn't have to put on too much of an act. As long as Serena stood and looked decorative, nobody expected much more of her, but when Candace and Richard insisted on going out to dinner together it was more difficult.

'Have you and Leo had a row?' Candace asked in the Ladies.

Serena concentrated on combing her hair. 'What makes you think that?'

'Just the way you're looking at each other.'

'I don't look at Leo in any special way.'

'Yes, you do, and Leo's exactly the same—as if he doesn't know whether to kiss you or shake you.' Candace leant closer to the mirror to touch up her lipstick. 'Being in love isn't always as easy as it looks, is it?'

To her horror, Serena felt her mouth work convulsively and she had to bite down hard on her bottom lip to stop it trembling. She put her comb away in her bag very carefully. 'No,' she said in a low voice. 'It's not easy.'

Candace glanced at her friend's averted face. 'Don't worry,' she said reassuringly. 'It'll be all right. Leo's obviously madly in love with you. You'll kiss and make up tonight.'

Only they wouldn't, Serena thought bleakly. They would drive home in silence as they did every time, and Leo wouldn't even look at her as she got out of the car. There would be no kiss to send her smiling to sleep. Instead she would lie alone in her empty bed. The treacherous memories would come whispering back, reminding her of Leo's lips against her breast, his hand gentling down her spine and curving over her hip, and, instead of the soft sighs of love, the room would echo only to the muffled sound of her crying helplessly into her pillow.

CHAPTER NINE

By the time they finally left for Yorkshire, Serena was so desperate that anything seemed preferable to continuing in what had become an intolerable situation. They left London at three o'clock on the Friday afternoon, setting out straight from the bank, but it wasn't early enough to stop them getting embroiled in the weekend rush. It was a bad start to a worse journey. Road-works made the heavy traffic even slower and as they sat in yet another tailback on the motorway it started to pour with rain.

It took them five hours to reach Leeds, five hours of rigid silence. Leo drove grim-faced, his hands so tight on the wheel that his knuckles showed white. Serena sat miserably beside him, staring out of her window at the other cars, which all seemed to be full of people talking and laughing together. She was taut with nerves, terrified of being so close to him for so long in case she gave in to the overwhelming urge to reach out and touch him. As so often before, she took refuge in prickly hostility in the hope that it would disguise her real feelings.

'You'd better navigate,' said Leo brusquely as they drove into another traffic jam just outside Leeds. He reached across her to pull a road atlas out of the glovebox, and Serena pressed herself back into her seat so that he wouldn't have to touch her. He only gave her a sardonic look as he dropped the atlas into her lap. 'We're trying to get to a place called Coggleston. Bill says it's north of Skipton somewhere.'

Serena studied the map for a while. 'I can't see it.'

'Have you tried the index?'

She glared at his tone but turned to the back, running her finger sullenly down the Cs. 'Here it is. . .sixty-two, D3.' She found the map again. 'Oh, I see. . .it's miles from Skipton!'

'Just tell me how to get there!' said Leo through his teeth.

Serena consulted the map again. 'We need the A65.' Easy enough to say, but the signs kept disappearing and the pelting rain made it difficult to see through the frantic whack and thump of the windscreen-wipers. They ended up driving in circles around the outskirts of Leeds while both their tempers wore extremely thin. Nor did things improve when they finally made it to Skipton and then had to sit behind a slowly swaying truck for miles along winding roads.

'We should have gone right there,' said Serena, just as Leo managed to overtake it.

He swore under his breath. 'I need a little more notice!'

'How am I supposed to know where the turning is?' she ruffled up immediately. 'If you didn't drive so fast, I might be able to read the signposts!'

'If I drive any slower, we won't get there until Monday,' snarled Leo, spotting another right turn and turning abruptly into it with a squeal of tyres. 'We must be able to get back to that other road from here. See where they join up.'

Serena's eyes were having trouble focusing on the page on the rougher road. 'Er. . .I don't think they meet at all unless we can take a single track road which should be up here somewhere. I don't know where it'll be marked to; it doesn't seem to lead anywhere except this other road.'

'Can we get back to the first road or not?' Leo

demanded in exasperation. 'God, it's not that difficult to read a map, is it?'

'You read it if you're so clever!' snapped Serena, then pointed. 'This must be the track here,' she said as Leo shot past the turning.

He jammed on the brakes and the car jerked to a halt. Muttering, he threw an arm across the back of her seat and turned to reverse back to the turning. 'I hope you're right,' he said with a nasty look as he turned the car into the narrow entrance.

Serena's confidence began to evaporate as the road got narrower and narrower and steeper and steeper. The rain crashed on to the roof and Leo had to crawl along to avoid the sheep that suddenly emerged out of the gloom in the middle of the road. They did eventually make it back to the right road, but got lost another five times before they finally reached Coggleston, by which time they were both in a filthy mood after snapping and sniping at each other consistently.

'I'm surprised you manage to find your way around a kitchen,' gibed Leo as the car snarled to a halt on the gravel outside Coggleston Hall at last. 'You couldn't navigate your way out of a paper bag!'

'And it's a mystery to me how you run a bank when you lose your cool over a little thing like driving!' retorted Serena, getting out and slamming the door behind her before stalking across to the front door.

Leo caught up with her as she rang the bell. 'Don't spoil everything now,' he warned her. 'All we have to do is get through this weekend. Just remember how in love we're supposed to be!'

'Oh, shut up!' said Serena just before the front door opened, throwing out a glow of welcoming light through the rain. They both pinned on identically fixed smiles as Bill Redmayne appeared.

'I see it's turning into a typical English summer,' he

said, giving Serena a welcoming kiss. 'Did you have a terrible drive?'

'Let's say it was rather fraught,' said Leo, who was still looking tight-lipped in spite of his smile. 'I'm sorry we're late. We had a little trouble finding you.'

'Did you?' Bill looked surprised. 'It's a perfectly straightforward route from Skipton.'

'My navigator opted for the picturesque route.' Leo was unable to prevent casting an unpleasant look at Serena, who smiled brittly back.

'Had a tiff, have you?' Bill gave a guffaw of laughter. 'You'll feel better after a drink and a good meal. I dare say you'll want to wash first, so I'll get Dorothy to show you to your room, then you can come and join us when you're ready.'

He handed them over to a pleasant-faced housekeeper, and nodded with gruff good humour at Serena. 'I may be old-fashioned about a lot of things, but I know how things are nowadays so we've put you in together. It was easy to see how you two felt about each other, and there's nothing worse than guests tiptoeing up and down the corridors all night. It wakes the dogs.'

Serena avoided looking at Leo as they followed Dorothy up the stairs to a large, luxurious room. She pointed out the *en-suite* bathroom, smiled, and left them staring in consternation at the double bed.

It was Leo who moved first, taking off his jacket and hanging it in the wardrobe. 'We'd better not keep them waiting.'

'What are you going to do about the bed?' she asked, finding her voice. Sharing a room in twin beds would have been bad enough, but sharing a bed would be torture.

'What do you expect me to do about it?' said Leo in a hard voice. 'Go down and tell Bill that my fiancée doesn't want to sleep with me and could we have separate bedrooms, please?'

'It's not unheard of,' said Serena tightly. 'You could tell him you respect me too much to sleep with me before we're married or something.'

'Ha!' scoffed Leo. 'Very convincing!'

'Well, what do you suggest?'

'I *suggest* that you think of the money and make the best of it. I don't intend to make a fool of myself in front of Bill Redmayne at this stage. We're both sleeping in this room, and I for one am sleeping in the bed. If you want to share it with me, fine. If not, you can sleep on the floor.'

'Very chivalrous!' snapped Serena.

Leo headed for the bathroom. 'I don't see why I should spend an uncomfortable night just because you've suddenly developed maidenly scruples. It didn't bother you before,' he added unkindly.

Serena flushed and set her teeth. 'That was different.'

'Was it?' he jeered.

'You know it was,' she said in a low voice.

There was a tight pause, then he turned away once more. 'You're getting paid for both occasions, so you'll have to just put up with it, won't you? If it's any comfort, I'm not exactly thrilled at the prospect of sleeping with you either!'

Serena dumped her case on the bed and began angrily searching for her wash-bag. 'I wish I'd never agreed to this stupid charade!'

'It's worked, hasn't it?' said Leo from his bathroom. He had stripped off his shirt and was washing his face vigorously, but they were both so cross that they had forgotten to feel awkward about the inevitable intimacy of the situation. 'Noelle seems to have got the message, the merger looks promising and you're getting paid. I don't know what you're complaining about. Few people get the chance to earn that much money so easily.'

'Easily! I don't call putting up with your arrogance and rudeness easy!' She was unpacking wildly, throwing her clothes over the bed. 'I've stood around at boring receptions and been pleasant to a lot of boring people talking about boring money—I don't call that easy either. Nor is it much fun being driven around by a bad-tempered maniac in the rain, or having to share a bed with a man who's selfish and narrow-minded and obnoxious and. . .and. . .a pig!'

Leo came out of the bathroom scowling, rubbing his face with a towel. The hair on his forehead was wet and spiky and Serena had a terrifying urge to run her fingers through it and smooth it back into shape. She turned sharply away, snatching up her wash-bag and stalking to the bathroom where she slammed the door closed.

'Don't you think you're being a little childish?' he shouted through it.

'No, I don't! I've had enough of being snapped at and lectured and patronised. If I want to sulk, I will!'

'Well, don't sulk too long. They're waiting for us downstairs, and I'm starving.'

Serena wanted nothing more than to be left alone with her bad mood and a nice long bath, but she had to make do with washing her face and brushing her teeth, which was at least an improvement. Leo was standing in front of the mirror knotting his tie when she marched out of the bathroom. He had been more successful than she had in controlling his temper. There was still a certain rigidity about his jaw, but otherwise he looked infuriatingly calm and cool and stomach-churningly attractive, and not at all like a man who had had a long, frustrating drive through the rain with an argumentative fiancée. Serena felt like a limp rag next to him.

Turning her back ostentatiously, she pulled off her

shirt and suede skirt and stepped into a pair of black silk trousers that made her long legs look longer than ever. With it she wore a white silk top and a wide belt patterned in gold. She was fastening this around her waist when she glanced round and saw that Leo was watching her in the mirror as he adjusted his cuffs.

Time slowed until it stopped altogether, and her hands stilled at her belt as the air evaporated from her lungs. The terrible tension and hostility drained away, leaving the two of them staring at each other in the mirror while the silence stretched and tightened with an entirely new current of awareness.

Serena could feel her heart beat with a slow, hypnotic thud of temptation. She could walk up to Leo and put her arms around his waist, lean her cheek against his back. She could tell him that she hadn't meant anything she had said, that she loved him and wished they could stay here with the inviting-looking bed instead of going downstairs to make polite conversation.

She could, but she wouldn't.

It took an immense effort to tear her eyes away and fumble for her hairbrush. Bending over, glad of the excuse to hide her face, she brushed out the thick copper hair until it shone, and by the time she had straightened, tossing it back over her shoulders, Leo was shrugging on his jacket, his expression so cold that she wondered if she had imagined the look in his eyes just now. Had it been no more than a trick of the light?

Horrified at how close she had come to revealing herself, she fixed in a pair of huge gold earrings and concentrated on applying a bold red lipstick. Her eyes looked very green in the mirror. Leo had said they just had to get through the weekend and then it would be over. She couldn't risk letting her guard down now.

Downstairs, they found the others in the sitting-room where they had obviously been having a few drinks while they waited for them. Oliver leapt up and greeted Serena like an old friend, while Noelle was predictably cooler. She introduced them to a suavely charming stockbroker called Philip. Like Leo, he was dark and attractive and exuded an indefinable air of wealth, but he lacked Leo's magnetic quality. It was like looking at a pale negative of him.

It hadn't taken Noelle long to find a substitute for Leo, Serena thought, accepting a drink, but as the evening wore on she began to wonder if Noelle too was finding Philip a poor imitation compared to the reality. She certainly seemed to devote herself to Leo, who made absolutely no effort to discourage her. Perhaps he thought that now the merger seemed virtually certain he could afford to get involved with Noelle after all, knowing that by the time she got round to suggesting marriage the deal would have gone through?

She wasn't the only one to notice Noelle's interest. Once or twice Serena caught Philip looking disconsolate, and she sent him a sympathetic smile. She knew how he felt. Leo had obviously set out to make himself charming and his smile kept burning at the edge of her eyes as she tried to talk to Bill and Oliver. She couldn't stop thinking about his mouth and his hands and what it would be like to lie next to him and not be able to touch him. She was terrified that her treacherous body would betray her, and she was stiff with nerves by the time they all said goodnight on the landing.

The bed loomed out at her as they went into the room, and the click as Leo closed the door seemed very loud in the taut silence. 'You use the bathroom first,' he said in a cool, impersonal voice. Clearly he wasn't bothered by the prospect of sleeping next to her!

Serena shut herself in the bathroom, willing her hands to stop shaking. This was ridiculous. There was absolutely nothing to be nervous about. Leo was probably already planning his seduction of Noelle, so he was hardly likely to try and touch *her*. All she had to do was get into bed, ignore him and go to sleep.

Easy.

She was passionately grateful that the cool change in the weather had reminded her to bring a nightdress with her. It was reassuringly old-fashioned, with long sleeves and a demure bodice that laced up the front, and fell modestly to her toes. At least Leo couldn't accuse her of trying to tempt him in this!

If only she didn't feel so. . .hot. Her whole body was strumming at the prospect of climbing into bed beside him and she was preternaturally aware of every whisper of sensation: the cool tiles beneath her feet, the feel of her hair against her cheek, the soft cotton brushing against her skin, her body aching with the memory of Leo's smile, his mouth drifting over her breast, his hands hard and insistent on her curves. . .

Stop it, stop it, stop it! She splashed cold water over her face again and straightened with a deep breath. At the bathroom door she hesitated for a long moment, her fingers around the handle, before she turned it and walked deliberately over to the bed. Leo was sitting on the edge, wearing only his trousers, bare-backed, as he took off his shoes and socks. He cast an ironic glance over his shoulder as she lifted the duvet and slid beneath it, drawing it up to her chin and lying as far to the edge of the bed as she could go without falling out, but he said nothing as he disappeared into the bathroom in his turn.

When he came out, Serena stiffened. Closing her eyes and pretending to be asleep, she lay rigid, but he ignored her anyway, switching off the overhead light and walking round to his side of the bed as if she weren't even there. She heard the click of the bedside lamp being switched off, then the creak and dip of the bed as he got in and settled himself comfortably. He didn't even say goodnight.

She listened tensely to the sound of his breathing, enraged when she heard it change as he slipped effortlessly into sleep. How could he be relaxed enough to fall asleep? Didn't he remember the last time they had shared a bed, when they had fallen across it laughing breathlessly, kissing, their hands moving over each other in eager, urgent discovery?

At least she could relax now that he was sleeping. She eased herself cautiously away from her position clinging to the edge of the bed. She wasn't touching him but it was impossible to ignore his warm, steadily breathing presence only inches away.

It seemed to Serena that she lay awake for hours staring up at the ceiling and resisting the urge to roll over and snuggle up against the hard comfort of Leo's body, but it was probably only a matter of minutes before the long journey took its toll and sleep stole over her.

She woke next morning to the feel of Leo stirring against her. At some time during the night they must have rolled together, for he was lying on his front, his face pressed into her throat and his arm heavy across her. Serena's own arm was hooked around his neck, the other flung up on to the pillow.

She blinked sleepily as Leo sighed and kissed her neck with a mumbled endearment before raising his head to look down into her face. Still half tangled in dreams, she smiled up into grey eyes that were alight with warmth.

'Serena,' he breathed, and bent to seek her mouth with his own, but just as he would have found it he seemed to hear the echo of his own voice. His lips were almost touching hers, her arm was tightening around his neck, pulling him down to her. 'Serena?' he said again, and she felt him stiffen as cold reality filtered through the warmth of sleep. She saw the familiar contempt dawn in his eyes and her arm fell from his neck as they stared at each other in horrified recognition of what had so nearly happened.

Abruptly, Leo levered himself away from her. Unable to think of anything to say, Serena watched the rigid line of his spine as he sat on the edge of the bed and stared at the wall, then he got up and walked to the bathroom, closing the door carefully behind him.

Squeezing her eyes shut, she rolled on to her side and willed herself not to cry. Tense with unshed tears, she lay motionless as Leo came out of the bathroom, dressed, and left the room without saying a word. Only then did she get up. Numbly, she went through the routine of bathing and dressing. All she had to do was get through this weekend. She chanted the words like a mantra as she pulled on black trousers and an olive-green shirt.

At breakfast, Bill announced that he wanted to talk to Leo. 'Oliver, you'll look after Serena, won't you?'

'Delighted to,' said Oliver promptly. 'It's such a nice day, we could walk over to Malham and have lunch in a pub. These two will be talking business all day. What do you say?'

Serena glanced at Leo. He was smiling at something Noelle was saying, patently uninterested in what she was going to be doing. 'That sounds lovely,' she replied warmly.

'Good,' said Oliver, smiling at her. 'What about you and Philip, Noelle? Do you want to come with us?'

'Oh, no, I don't think so,' said Noelle vaguely. 'You and Serena go.'

Leo disappeared into the study with Bill without bothering to say goodbye as Serena set out with Oliver. Last night's rain had vanished, leaving the sky a fresh, laundered blue, and the hills stood out against it with a new clarity. Everything seemed sharp and distinct in the morning air. The grass was an astonishing green, scattered with sheep that looked as newly washed as the sky, and divided by neat stone walls.

Serena hardly noticed. She looked at the wild flowers drifting colour along the roadside, at the moss on a five-bar gate and the tussocky grass beneath her feet as they climbed, but all she saw was the expression in Leo's eyes as he had remembered that he didn't want to kiss her after all.

The brisk walk brought colour to her cheeks, though, and gradually the exhilaratingly clear air and the beauty of the hills began to have their effect. She was being utterly pathetic about Leo, she realised with a touch of her old astringency. Why was she moping around feeling miserable and resentful when she should be grateful that she had faced the truth before she had made a complete fool of herself? She should be making plans instead of simply wishing things could be different.

Really, she was ashamed of herself, she thought, toiling up to the top of the hill. She had always been so strong until now. When she had discovered the truth about Alex, she had picked herself up and mentally brushed herself down before concentrating fiercely on the future. Surely she could do the same again? She had survived before; she would survive this time.

Oliver's undisguised admiration was balm for her wounded feelings. Convinced that his father would agree to the merger, he was full of plans for his country club, and eager for Serena's advice on the catering side. 'I wouldn't have a clue about cooking,' he told her. 'My role will be strictly front of house, so I'll be on the look-out for a good cook—so if you know of anyone let me know.'

They had lunch sitting outside a pub in the sunshine, and Serena refused to admit to herself that she was missing Leo. Oliver was much nicer, anyway, she told herself. He was charming and attentive and interested in her. . .it was just that he didn't have Leo's mouth or Leo's hands and when she looked at him her insides didn't twist and wrench with longing.

It was five o'clock before they arrived back at Coggleston Hall, and there was no sign of either Leo or Noelle. 'They went out for a walk,' said Philip, trying to sound as if he didn't care. 'Noelle said she wanted to discuss some business with Leo.'

Serena could imagine what kind of business Noelle had in mind! Gritting her teeth as she showered and changed, she told herself again and again that she didn't care. She was brushing her hair by the window when she saw them strolling up the drive together. They moved slowly, intimately, deep in conversation, and Serena's fingers tightened around her brush. If Leo wanted to forget his precious charade, that was fine by her!

She managed to avoid being alone with him all evening. Over drinks, Bill announced that he had agreed to the merger. Oliver gave a whoop of delight while Noelle jumped up and kissed her father. Serena looked at Leo. For a man who had achieved exactly what he wanted, his smile was forced and he deliberately avoided her eye. Feeling that at least one of them ought to make the effort to look pleased, Serena smiled. 'That's wonderful news!'

Dinner seemed to last forever. Oliver talked excitedly about the country club and told his father about all the suggestions Serena had made. Leo looked increasingly boot-faced as Oliver enthused about her contribution but Serena only tilted her chin at him. He had made his choice. If he was going to slope off for secret strolls with Noelle that was his business, but there was no call for him to glower at her. *She* hadn't forgotten that they were supposed to be engaged!

The blacker Leo looked, the more Serena sparkled. She was determined to show him that she couldn't care less what he had been doing with Noelle. Never had she been such scintillating company. She kept Bill and Oliver guffawing with laughter and even Philip began to look more cheerful. She felt quite exhausted by the time they reached the coffee stage, but it had been worth it to see the muscle twitching convulsively in Leo's jaw. He had devoted himself to Noelle, but she knew that he had been listening to every word.

'I hope you're ashamed of your little performance tonight,' he snarled when he finally managed to drag her upstairs. He practically pushed her into the bedroom.

'What performance?' said Serena insultingly.

'You know perfectly well! Hogging the limelight, fluttering those long eyelashes of yours, dropping all those hints to Oliver. . .you're supposed to be *my* fiancée!'

'Only when it suits you! In case you've forgotten, you're supposed to be my fiancé too, but no one would have guessed from the way you carried on today! You hardly said a word to me at breakfast, you showed absolutely no interest in what I was going to do for the day while you were shut up in your meeting—you couldn't even be bothered to say goodbye!

'And is my loving fiancé waiting anxiously for my return? Of course not! He's off enjoying a cosy tête-à-tête with Noelle! You complain about my performance but it's yours you should be ashamed of!'

'We were taking business.'

'Oh, *sure*!' Serena was slamming around the bathroom, too angry to feel self-conscious about getting ready for bed tonight.

'It's true—she wanted to know if there would be a position for her in the merged bank.'

'Flat on her back, I suppose?'

'Don't be crude, Serena. It doesn't suit you.'

'Nothing about this situation *suits* me! I thought you wanted to put her off you? She'd obviously turned her attention to Philip until you turned up and started whispering to her over the dinner-table and taking off for little walks. You've hardly talked to anyone else all weekend!'

'And whose fault is that?' demanded Leo indistinctly as he brushed his teeth with the same complete absence of awkwardness. 'You haven't stopped talking long enough to let anyone else get a word in edgeways. Of course I had to talk to her! I could hardly ignore her while you held court, especially when you seemed bent on spoiling things for her with Philip!'

'With *Philip*?' Serena gaped at him. She had pulled on her nightdress and was dragging a brush furiously through her hair. 'What are you talking about?'

'You know,' sneered Leo, unbuttoning his shirt as he came back into the bedroom. 'I saw all those little smiles you gave him last night, and you practically had him wrapped round your little finger by the end of this evening! Not content with ensuring that Oliver's besotted with you, you thought you'd work on Philip as well. I'm surprised you didn't just make a straight play for Bill! He's got more money than any of us, and he seems to be a big fan of yours—God knows why!'

Serena jerked back the duvet and bounced angrily into bed. 'Perhaps he sees me as a person instead of a means to an end!'

'Don't flatter yourself!' Leo snapped off the overhead light and got in beside her. They faced each other furiously in the light of the bedside lamp. 'The way you were flaunting yourself tonight, I would be very surprised if any of them were interested in your mind.'

'Whereas you're fascinated by Noelle's towering intellect, I suppose?'

'At least she's got enough sense not to make an exhibition of herself!'

She glared at him. 'If she's so marvellous, why are you here?'

'You know why.'

'After the way you've been carrying on with Noelle, I'm not sure I do any more!' Serena took one of the pillows and shoved it under the duvet between them before throwing herself down with her back to him. 'You seem to have all sorts of strange reasons for getting into bed with me!'

'What exactly do you mean by that?' asked Leo menacingly.

She jerked round to face him once more, too flushed with the quarrel to ignore him as she had wanted. 'Why did you sleep with me before?' she demanded. 'Because you didn't have anything better to do that night? Because you thought it would make me stick to your precious agreement?'

'Because we both wanted each other that night,' he said. There was a dangerous stillness about him but Serena had gone too far to heed the warning.

'Oh, really?' she exclaimed sarcastically. 'That's interesting! I thought I was supposed to have seduced you for the money.'

'I don't think the money occurred to you till the next morning and then it was too good an opportunity to pass up, but you wanted me that night. You said so.'

'In that case I was lying!' declared Serena, stormy-eyed.

'No, you weren't. For once, you were telling the

truth. You wanted me then, and what's more,' he said, dragging the pillow out from between them and chucking it on the floor, 'you want me now.'

'That's what you think!'

Serena began to sit up, but Leo pulled her back and rolled over to pin her beneath him. 'Why don't we just put it to the test?' he suggested.

If he had been rough, or demanding, she would have been able to resist. If he had tried to force her, she would have fought him to the end. But he didn't. He kissed her ear very softly, then began to drop featherlight kisses along her jaw towards her mouth, and all the time he held himself braced above her so that she could easily push him away.

She got as far as raising her hands to his chest. She was going to shove him away but he had reached her lips and was kissing her with a tenderness that melted her bones, dissolving the last flimsy barriers of her resistance like the last patch of snow in the sunshine. Deliberately, he kept his hands on either side of her while his mouth alone sought and found the sweetness of her response, and only when Serena succumbed with a sigh of release to the promise of a joy she might never know again did he reach for the laces at the front of her nightdress.

He kept their kisses slow and sweet as he let his hand drift down to the hem and slide in a lingering caress up the silken length of her leg, rucking up the soft cotton. It was Serena who pulled the nightdress over her head and tossed it aside, she who reached for him and murmured with pleasure as he secured her against the sleekness of his bare skin, and it was she too who cried out first as he took her with infinite care along paths of delight to the explosion of ecstasy that was waiting for them both at the end.

CHAPTER TEN

THE morning sun woke Serena. They had been so angry last night that they had forgotten to draw the curtains, and she lay for a while, watching the motes drifting in the beams of sunlight and savouring the feel of Leo's body, warm and relaxed against her.

He was still sleeping soundly, one arm thrown possessively across her, and she stroked his hair tenderly before she disentangled herself. He stirred as she slid from beneath him, and his arm tightened instinctively around her with an incoherent murmur of protest before he relaxed back into sleep.

She stood by the bed, looking down on him. In sleep, his face had lost the guarded expression that so often looked like arrogance, and he seemed younger, less invulnerable. She wished she could slip back into bed beside him and kiss him awake. . .but hadn't she decided to stop wishing? Last night had changed nothing. He had talked of desire but not of love, and Serena knew that desire meant nothing without it.

No, far better to pretend that last night had never happened. Leo would take her home today and that would be that. She would have to learn to live without him some time, and the sooner she started the better.

Very gently, she bent down and kissed the corner of his mouth. It might be the only chance she had to say goodbye the way she wanted.

It was very early. Her feet left footprints in the dew as she walked across the grass and up through the trees to the hill behind the hall. She sat for a while at the top, thinking about the way Leo had made love to her.

It had been so sweet, so right between them that it was hard to believe that he felt nothing for her.

But they couldn't spend their whole time in bed. There was too much dividing them in the cold light of day, and clinging to Leo in the hope that he might one day decide to commit himself would only bring her more heartache. It was much wiser to accept that today was the end. Harder, but wiser.

On her way back down the hill, she met Oliver. 'You're up early,' he called, breathing heavily as he came up to her.

'So are you,' said Serena with a rather strained smile. She didn't want to talk to him about what she had been doing sitting alone on top of the hill, but she needn't have worried. He was still obsessed with his country club.

'I couldn't sleep,' he told her. 'I've got too many plans chasing each other round my mind. I came up with several new ideas last night, too.' He talked on about them as he turned and walked back down the hill with Serena, who listened and nodded and tried not to think about Leo.

At the bottom of the hill, a five-bar gate led into a wooded lane. They leant on it for a while, watching a small grey rabbit warming itself in a patch of sunlight.

'I wish I could have met you before Leo did,' Oliver burst out suddenly, and Serena stared at him in astonishment, taken aback by the sincerity in his voice. 'I really need someone like you,' he explained with a slightly shamefaced look. 'Someone strong and practical—and fun.

'Father never likes anyone, but he absolutely adores you. I've never seen him laugh like he did last night. I know he wishes I'd marry a girl like you. . . Oh, don't worry,' he hastened to reassure her as she opened her mouth to speak. 'I know you don't have eyes for anyone else but Leo. Even when you're not looking at each other, there's a sort of current between you. I noticed it the first time I met you, and that night we came to dinner it was obvious that you could hardly keep your hands off each other.

'Noelle rather fancied herself as Mrs Kerslake for a while, but she realised then that she didn't stand a chance against you. That's why she took up with Philip. He's been hanging around for ages, hoping she'd notice him. Leo's getting engaged to you was probably the best thing that could have happened to her!'

'She and Leo still seem to get on well together.' Serena couldn't prevent the note of jealousy in her voice.

'That's because she's decided she wants a position in the bank. Noelle's a lot smarter than she looks, and she knows Leo won't look at her now he's got you. I think she hoped for a while that I might cut Leo out but there isn't any chance of that. . .is there?' He looked at her half hopefully but mustered a smile when Serena shook her head.

'I'm sorry,' she said. She knew he would be thinking about the way she had flirted with him last night. She *had* encouraged him, she realised guiltily.

'Don't worry, I always knew that. . .really.' Oliver made a determined effort to sound cheerful. 'Well, if you can't fall in love with me, could you do me a favour instead?'

'Of course. . .if I can.'

'I think I've found the perfect place for the club, but I'd really appreciate your opinion. Come and look at it now!'

'Now?' said Serena, surprised.

'It's only ten minutes' drive away. We can be there and back before anyone else is up.'

Serena didn't really want to go, but she didn't know

how to refuse, and she was still feeling guilty about the way she had used him.

Oliver's estimate of the time it would take to get there proved to be somewhat optimistic. It was at least twenty-five minutes before they reached the old house he had found. It had been gutted by fire, but he showed Serena proudly round the ruins as if it were a national monument. She was appalled at how much work needed to be done, but the prospect didn't seem to deter Oliver and she had to agree that the setting was marvellous.

She kept glancing surreptitiously at her watch, but Oliver was in full flight, and by the time he eventually took her back to Coggleston Hall, the others were all sitting round the breakfast-table.

They all looked up as Serena and Oliver came in, except Leo, who carried on buttering his toast and didn't even glance at Serena. Well, what had she expected? That last night would make him miraculously fall in love with her after all? She sat down opposite him and let Noelle pour her a cup of coffee.

The other girl seemed much more cordial this morning. Serena wondered suspiciously if it was because of her walk with Leo yesterday. Could he possibly have told her the truth after all? There would be no need for Noelle to resent her if she knew that the engagement had never been real. Serena sipped her coffee miserably, torturing herself with visions of Leo welcoming Noelle into a future in which she herself had no part.

Oliver was shaking some cereal into a bowl, enthusing about the site he had found as if Serena's approval was all he had been waiting for. 'She's been absolutely marvellous!' he told Leo. 'She's given me some fantastic ideas this morning. I've told her that if she ever gets bored with being married to you she can come into partnership with me!'

His jovial attempt to bring Leo into the conversation fell completely flat. Leo glanced at him, and then at Serena, patently unamused. 'Really?' he said, in such a glacial tone that there was an awkward silence.

Bill broke it. 'Well, what's everyone going to do today?'

'I'm afraid we must go,' said Leo brusquely.

'But you'll stay for lunch, surely?'

'We have to get back,' he insisted, curt to the point of rudeness.

Embarrassed, Serena felt obliged to be a little more grateful. 'It's been a lovely weekend,' she told Bill. 'I really am sorry we can't stay a bit longer.'

'There'll be plenty of other weekends,' said Bill, mollified. 'I hope we'll see you up here often.'

He hugged her and repeated the invitation as they left. Noelle, Serena noticed darkly, was positively pleasant as she and Philip said goodbye. Ignoring Leo's wintry expression, Oliver kissed Serena warmly just before she got into the car. 'Thank you for everything, Serena, and come again soon!'

Leo didn't even wait until the end of the drive before he started. He had prowled around the room as she'd packed, simmering with suppressed rage. He was obviously dying for a fight. Serena had ignored him, determined not to give him the satisfaction of asking him what the matter was. He was bound to tell her anyway.

And she was right.

'I'd have thought you would have had the decency to wait one more day before you started feathering yet another nest for the future!' he said savagely.

Well, if he wanted a fight, he could have one! 'Do I have to guess, or are you going to tell me what you're talking about?'

'I'm talking about the clever way you played Oliver

Redmayne,' he snarled. 'Of course, I was the one who told you how rich Bill was, so who could be more useful to you than his only son? That way you get a limitless source of money *and* Oliver's bloody country club thrown into the bargain! I'm sure it won't take you long to turn that into the restaurant you've always wanted!'

'I haven't got the slightest interest in Oliver's club!'

'It's just the money, is it?' said Leo unpleasantly. 'Perhaps I was wrong. Perhaps all that interest in his club was just a way to worm your way closer to his bank account. It's worked too. "She's been absolutely marvellous!"' He mimicked Oliver's drawl with uncanny accuracy. '"She's given me some fantastic ideas. . .". I'll bet you have! It doesn't take much to work out what sort of ideas you came up with during your cosy little assignation this morning!'

'It takes more than you've got, obviously!' Serena said furiously. She was shaking with anger. 'And it was not an assignation! I met Oliver quite by chance this morning. He asked if I'd give him my opinion on the site he'd found, and I could hardly refuse.'

'Do you really expect me to believe that? You spent the entire day with him yesterday, flirted with him all evening and then met him this morning *by chance*?'

'I don't give a damn whether you believe me or not!' snapped Serena.

'Oh, I believe *that* all right!' Leo was driving with a cold, concentrated fury. 'If I had any fellow-feeling at all, I'd warn Oliver what he was letting himself in for. He won't stand a chance with you as his "partner"!' He managed to put insulting inverted commas around the word. 'You'll trample all over him, use him for what you can, then move on—just like you've done with me!'

'With *you*. . .!' Serena struggled for words to express her astonishment. 'I don't believe I'm hearing this! You know more about using people than anyone else I know. What do you call the way you've treated me?'

'We had an agreement,' said Leo. 'You hung out for what you wanted and went into it with your eyes open. In view of the extortionate sum of money you screwed out of me I don't think you're in a position to complain about being used, but Oliver will be if you go into partnership with him.'

'Who says I am?'

'Are you?' he asked, as if the question was forced out of him. They had reached the main road, and he put his foot down on the accelerator. The car shot forward.

'I might,' said Serena provocatively. 'I'll need to do something after all, since I no longer have a job at Erskine Brookes.'

'You've had so much money out of me that you won't need a job!'

'Who's talking about money? I'm looking forward to a stimulating job, working with someone like Oliver who's kind and considerate and charming. I can tell you that both will make a nice change from the last few weeks!'

'You'll be bored within five minutes!'

'Oh, I don't know. . .think what fun I'll have spending all the money I've had from you!'

It was deliberately provocative, and Serena wasn't surprised that it earned her a diatribe from Leo about grasping, avaricious women, but by the time they reached Leeds she had had enough.

'Turn off here,' she interrupted him in mid-harangue as they passed a sign warning them of the turn-off for the city centre.

'Turn off? Why?'

'Because I'm not putting up with this any longer.

You can take me to the station and I'll wait for the next train to London.'

'Don't be absurd!'

'I've never been more serious in my life,' she told him. 'Quite apart from the fact that I have no intention of spending the next three hours listening to you being unpleasant and unreasonable, you're driving far too fast. Turning us both into a traffic statistic might relieve your temper but it won't do anything for mine. I'd feel safer on the train!'

Leo's hands tightened on the wheel and his jaw clenched so hard that Serena though he was going to explode. 'Very well,' he said in an icy voice after a monumental battle for control. 'If that's what you want.'

'It is.'

Snapping on the indicator with a vicious flick of his finger, Leo turned towards the city centre and drove her to the station without another word. 'I suppose you want your final payment?' he said tightly as they drew up outside.

Serena had forgotten all about it. She was about to tell him what he could do with his money when she remembered Madeleine. Bobby had been recovering well from his operation but he was still in hospital and, until he was quite out of danger, she couldn't afford to sacrifice money that might save him to her own pride.

'I certainly intend to claim what's due,' she told him coolly, unclicking her seatbelt. 'But it can wait until next week.'

'No, we'll finish this now,' said Leo. There was a taut look to his mouth as he reached for his cheque-book and scrawled out a cheque. He tossed it across to her with a sneer. 'At least this way I know there's no need for me to see or hear from you ever again.'

'No.' Quite cold, Serena took the cheque and put it

in her handbag. She got out of the car to retrieve her bag from the back and then came round to Leo's open window. 'I nearly forgot this,' she said, tugging the diamond engagement ring from her finger and dropping it into his lap as contemptuously as he had thrown the cheque to her. 'I'm sure you'll be able to sell this and recoup some of your expenses!' And, turning, she walked away from him without a backward look.

It was a long journey home. Serena stared blankly ahead of her and fought a rising sense of panic whenever she thought about life without Leo. She kept telling herself that she would never see him again and that she was glad, but her mind refused to accept it. He had become so much a part of her existence over the past few weeks that it was impossible to imagine what it would be like not to see him, to hear him, to touch him.

Her wretched temper! Too late she realised that if she had refused to respond to his taunts she might in the end have been able to make him see reason. He might never have come to love her, but at least she might have been able to see him occasionally. Wouldn't that have been better than facing the bleak emptiness that stretched ahead of her now?

It was hard now to believe why she had been so angry. Why hadn't she made him stop the car so that he could explain just why he was in such a fury? Why hadn't she just kissed him and let passion soothe the raw hurt between them as it had done last night?

It was too late now.

She moved through the next two days in a blur. She had no job to go to, nothing to take her mind from the ghastly treadmill of might-have-beens. All the clothes Leo had bought her were packed away, ready to be sent back to him, and the cheque lay untouched on the top. She was determined not to pay it into her account unless she really had to, but she would have to do something with it.

She rang Madeleine. Her sister sounded over the moon, a different woman from the one who had sobbed over the phone. 'I was going to ring you tonight!' she exclaimed. 'Bobby's home! He still needs to take it easy for a while, but the doctors say he's over the worst.'

'Oh, Madeleine, that's marvellous news!' Serena could forget her own misery listening to her sister's infectious delight.

'Isn't it? And there's something else I have to tell you, Serena. . .I'm getting married again!'

'What?'

Madeleine laughed. 'I thought you'd be surprised!'

Surprised! Serena felt as if she'd been hit by a sledge-hammer, but fortunately she didn't have to say anything as Madeleine chattered on.

'You remember I told you about my neighbour? Well, John's been incredible about looking after the boys while I've been at the hospital and we've ended up spending a lot of time together. He didn't say anything while I was so worried about Bobby, but last night he said it was time I had someone to look after me and he was going to be the one to do it. Oh, Serena, he's such a good, kind man. . .please say you're happy for me!'

'Of course I am,' she said, but Madeleine must have heard the doubt in her voice.

'I know you're thinking about Chris and how unhappy I was married to him, but marriage doesn't have to be like that. I was just unlucky that I didn't meet John a long time ago. He's good for me, Serena. He makes me feel safe and happy and secure, and he loves the boys.

'I told him how much you'd done for me, and he wants to send you back the money you sent me. He says he can afford to look after all of us now, and it sounded as if you could put the money to better use starting a restaurant like you've always wanted to do.'

'That's sweet of him,' said Serena, blinking away the tears. 'But don't let him do it, Madeleine. Get him to take you all away on holiday somewhere when Bobby's feeling better instead. It sounds as if you all deserve it!'

'Well, I'll let you argue it out with him when you meet him,' said Madeleine philosphically. 'I just wish you could find someone, Serena. You've no idea how nice it is to fall in love with someone who loves you!'

No, she had no idea what that was like. She only knew what it was like to fall hopelessly in love with an impossible dream. Serena was delighted that her sister was so happy, but when she had put the phone down the flat seemed bleaker and emptier than before.

She picked up the cheque and looked down at the scrawled signature for a moment, before tearing it deliberately in half and putting it in an envelope addressed to Leo and marked 'Personal'. Dropping it into the post-box at the end of the road, she decided that it marked a fitting end to the whole charade. Now she would put him out of her mind and start afresh.

It was easier said than done, but Serena tried hard. The very next day she made arrangements to put her flat on the market and began scouring catering magazines for jobs outside London. She considered Oliver's offer briefly, but knew that there would be too many memories of Leo in Yorkshire. She was looking for a job that was as far away from Leo as possible and hard enough to give her no time to think about him.

In the meantime, she went back to making soups. Soon she had so many in her freezer that she realised she would have to get rid of some before she simply ran out of space. On the off chance, she took some samples down to the delicatessen at the end of the road where they sold out on the first day.

If she wasn't careful she would end up with another business in London, she thought one evening as she stood and chopped carrots listlessly. She wasn't sure if she could bear the thought of bumping into Leo by accident, of seeing him with someone else. She wasn't sure she could bear the thought of not seeing him, either. She missed him with a physical ache.

She was stirring onions when the doorbell went three days later. She was tempted not to answer it. She didn't feel up to dealing with any salesman or some doorstep survey, but when the bell went again she sighed and gave in. Resting her wooden spoon across the top of the pan, she wiped her hands automatically on her apron and headed down the stairs.

She was framing a polite but firm refusal as she opened the door, but the words died on her lips when she saw who was standing on the step.

It was Leo. Looking ravaged by strain and exhaustion, but unmistakably Leo. The silver eyes were bleak and his mouth was set in a tired, anxious line that tore at Serena's heart, but it was him. It was really him.

Stunned, incredulous, uncertain whether to despair or rejoice, she clutched at the door for support for legs which threatened to fold beneath her. 'Wh—what are you doing here?' she whispered.

'I came to give you back the money you've earned,' said Leo, pulling the two halves of the cheque from his pocket and holding them out to her. His voice sounded creaky with disuse, as if talking was an effort, and he hadn't taken his eyes off her face.

Money. . .was that all he ever thought about? Serena closed her eyes despairingly against the temptation of throwing herself into his arms and begging him not to go away. She felt as if there was a tight band around her throat and she was terrified that she was going to burst into tears. 'I don't want your money,' she managed to say.

'You wanted it before,' he said harshly. 'You've already had ten thousand pounds. Why change your mind now, when you've earned another ten thousand?'

'I don't need it now,' Serena told him, summoning up some weary defiance. 'I don't need your money and I don't need you, any more than you need me.'

Leo looked down at the torn cheque in his hand and then back up at her, his eyes intensely light. 'But I do need you,' he corrected her.

Serena didn't think she could bear to go through the pretence again. Was that what he had come for, to offer her another role to play? Her legs were trembling, her knuckles white where she was still gripping the edge of the door. 'What's the matter?' she asked, clinging frantically to the dregs of her pride. 'Is Noelle still pressing for a wedding-ring?'

'No.' He shook his head. 'She's just announced her engagement to Philip.'

'Then why do you need a fiancée?'

'I don't,' said Leo. 'I need *you*. I need a girl with fierce green eyes and a stubborn chin and a shining smile, a girl who's turned my whole life upside-down.'

He was still standing on the step, making no move to touch her, but the expression in his eyes set hope beating an incredulous tattoo in her heart.

'I don't need you to save my freedom, Serena. I'm not sure that I ever did. All I need is to know that I can turn and find you there. When you walked away from me that day. . .' His smile twisted as he realised he had no words to describe how he had felt then. 'I've missed you,' he finished simply.

'But. . .but. . .' Serena couldn't take it in. She felt

very odd, as if none of this was happening to her. It was as if she were watching a film produced by some cruel trick of her imagination to taunt her with the impossible. 'You despise me,' she remembered, seizing on reality.

'I wanted to,' he said in a low voice. 'I pretended that I did. It was easier than admitting that I wanted to spend the rest of my life with a girl who made no secret of the fact that she despised *me*.'

Very slowly, Serena let go of the door and found that her legs would hold her after all. She shook her head, still half convinced that she was dreaming. 'I never despised you,' was all she could say.

'I gave you every reason to, I know.' Leo seemed daunted by her lack of response, but determined to finish what he had to say. How was he to know that she simply couldn't explain the emotions jumbling in her mind? 'I was horrible to you. I was callous and insulting and cruel, but it was only because I was half out of my mind with jealousy and despair because I didn't think you could ever love me the way I love you.'

'You love me?' Serena repeated in a whisper, hardly daring to believe that dreams could come true after all. 'You love *me*?'

'Yes.' She had never realised that the silver-grey eyes could look so warm. Reaching forward, he took her hands in his. 'I love you and I need you and I want you, and I'll do anything you ask, Serena, if only you'll let me try and make up for the way I've behaved towards you.' His grip tightened. 'Did you mean it when you said you didn't hate me?'

Serena nodded, a smile trembling on her lips as the last stone of misery shattered in a shock of happiness so intense it was almost painful. 'I was pretending too,' she confessed, and the smile that had started in his eyes spread slowly over his face.

'You were?'

'I've been pretending that all I wanted was my independence, that all that mattered was my pride,' she said quietly. 'But it didn't work because when I tried to pretend that I wasn't desperately, hopelessly in love with you I just couldn't.'

'Serena. . .' Leo's voice was ragged, his hands unsteady as he cupped her face wonderingly. 'Serena, do you really love me?'

'Yes,' she said, and her eyes shimmered green with tears of relief that she could stop pretending and tell the truth at last. 'Oh, yes, I do. . .I do. . .I can't tell how much I love you!'

'Then you'd better try and show me,' murmured Leo, smiling, and Serena smiled too, sliding her arms around his neck and pulling his head down so that she could kiss him in the way she had been wanting to do for so long. His lips were as warm and exciting as she remembered but loving him, knowing that he loved her, gave their kisses a piercing, inexpressible sweetness that left her dizzy with joy.

Leo's hands drifted from her face to her throat and down over her warm curves until he could fold her hard against him, and she clung to him as the sweetness spun into a frenzied desperation to make up for the time they had lost. Oblivious to the amused glances of passers-by, they stood on the doorstep and kissed deeply, hungrily, able at last to succumb to the passion they had both tried so hard to deny, and which needed to be denied no longer.

Serena held Leo tightly, murmuring his name breathlessly as he mumbled endearments into her hair. She had thought that she would never see him again and now he was here, hard and solid beneath her hands, kissing her almost frantically, her eyes, her ear, her throat, then her mouth again, as if he too had to reassure himself that she was real.

'Serena,' he sighed at last, resting his cheek against her bright hair, cradling her against him. 'I thought I'd never be able to kiss you again.'

'I know. . .I know.' Incoherent with happiness, she pressed her face into his throat and kissed the pulse beating below his ear. 'I've been so miserable without you.'

'I've been through every kind of hell since Sunday,' he said, tightening his arms around her, 'trying to tell myself I was well rid of you, longing to see you, convinced that I'd been so unpleasant you'd shut the door in my face.'

'What made you come today?'

'You sent back the cheque. I'd got beyond worrying about whether you wanted the money or not, but it was the perfect excuse to come and see you. Why did——?' He broke off and sniffed. 'Has passion really set us alight or is something burning?'

'My onions!' Tearing herself out of his arms, Serena raced upstairs, but it was too late. The onions were blackened and smoking and she hastily turned off the gas before throwing open a window to try and get rid of the smell.

'Disaster?' asked Leo, who had followed her more leisurely up the stairs, closing the door behind him.

Serena peered at the bottom of the pan. It would probably never be the same again but then, after this magical, wonderful morning, neither would she. She smiled at Leo. 'Not now you're here,' she said.

The smell of burnt onions was so strong that they closed the kitchen door and sought refuge in the sitting-room. Leo sat down on the sofa and pulled an unresisting Serena on to his lap. 'Why *did* you send back that cheque, Serena?'

'I didn't need it any more.' She told him everything then—about Madeleine's dependence on her, and Bobby's illness, and about how her sister had found someone else to look after her. 'I only took that cheque for Bobby,' she finished. 'I would never have used it for myself.'

Leo was horrified. 'You mean you've been worrying about your sister all this time? You let me accuse you of being mercenary, when all you were doing was supporting your family? Why didn't you tell me?'

'I should have done, I know, but I didn't want you to think I was begging for money.' She relaxed back against him with a rueful smile. 'My stupid pride!'

'*I'm* the one who's stupid,' Leo castigated himself. 'I should have guessed that you must have a good reason for wanting money. You've got such honest eyes,' he explained, touching her cheek. 'I should have known you couldn't be like all the other girls I'd known. I *did* know. You were so different from anyone else I'd ever met that it didn't feel right when it seemed as if you were just the same after all, but instead of following my instincts I told myself it just confirmed all my prejudices about mercenary women.'

'Why were you so bitter?' Serena asked. 'Not all women are like that.'

'For a long time it seemed as if they were,' said Leo. 'Coming back to take over the bank was a shock in more ways than one. All at once I found myself pursued by women who wouldn't have looked at me twice when I was working my way round the world.'

Serena stilled. 'Was there anyone special?'

'I thought she was special until I met you and knew what special really was,' said Leo, stroking her hair. 'At the time I thought I was madly in love with Donna. I met her in the States and she was so beautiful I fell for her like the proverbial ton of bricks, but, as she was only too ready to tell me, I wasn't nearly special enough for her. She didn't make any secret of the fact that she was looking for someone rich and powerful.'

He paused and his smile was rather twisted. 'I asked her to marry me and she laughed in my face. Now I realise what a lucky escape I had, but at the time I was devastated to realise that I'd been prepared to give up my freedom for someone who didn't even want me.

'In a way, Donna did me a favour,' he went on after another moment. 'She was the reason I decided to come home and make a success of the bank. I suppose I had some idea of proving myself, of showing her what she'd missed. The next time I saw her I was chairman of Erskine Brookes and visiting New York. Donna came to my hotel and more or less told me that she was available now that I had something to offer her. It should have been my moment of triumph but. . .'

'But what?' Serena prompted quietly.

Leo shrugged. 'Suddenly she didn't seem so beautiful any more. The whole incident left a sour taste in my mouth and I decided there and then that I didn't want anything to do with women who were only interested in my money. The more I met who were, the more cynical I became. . .and then I met you.' He smiled at her. 'I took one look into those fierce green eyes of yours and I was lost!'

'You never fell in love with me in that ghastly dress!' Serena protested with mock-indignation.

'I didn't even notice your dress,' Leo apologised. 'All I noticed were your eyes and your hair.' He kissed them in turn and let his lips travel down to her jaw. 'And the cross way you lifted your chin at me, of course!'

Lifting his head, he lovingly smoothed the coppery hair away from her face. 'You were so defiant, so different. . .and then you started talking about money and I thought that perhaps you weren't so different after all. I was disappointed, but I still changed my flight so that I could see you again that evening.'

Serena sat up in astonishment. 'You stayed to see *me*?'

'Oh, I gave myself some other reason, and nearly managed to convince myself that I wasn't the slightest bit interested in you, but you were impossible to ignore that night.'

He smiled at the memory and let his hand slide down her spine possessively and pull her back towards him. 'You were like a flame in that dress. You made everyone else look dull and insipid, and I was more intrigued than I wanted to admit. And when you kissed me I was more than intrigued—I was shocked at how much I wanted you.'

Serena had subsided back against his shoulder with a sigh of contentment. 'You certainly hid it well! You didn't look the least bit interested when we met in that lift!'

'That was because I was expecting to see you and I'd had time to put my guard up. I'd seen your name on the contract and I felt. . .I don't know. . .as if it was *meant*. I wasn't sure I liked the feeling of not being in control. I felt as if I was being dragged, kicking and screaming, into the very situation I had resisted for so long, and I was determined not to give in without a fight.'

He twisted a lock of shining hair around his fingers. 'I fought it as long as I could. I even told myself that asking you to act as my fiancée was a purely practical idea, when really it was the only way I could think of to spend more time with you. You hadn't made any secret of the fact that you didn't like me, and I knew you would probably refuse if I asked you out directly.'

'I probably would have,' Serena confessed. 'After

Alex, I was scared of getting involved, and I was nervous of the way you made me feel. I didn't want to fall in love with you, but I kept remembering the way you kissed me.' She eased herself away from his shoulder slightly so that she could look into his eyes. 'I'd never felt like that before, Leo.'

'I wish I'd known,' he said, with a smile and a kiss. 'It would have saved a lot of complications! As it was, I involved both of us in that ridiculous charade. It was a nasty shock when you coolly upped the stakes and demanded more money, just when I'd let myself be convinced that you weren't like all the other girls I knew.

'I felt as if you'd made a fool out of me,' he added honestly. 'I couldn't be sure about you after that. Whenever we seemed to be getting close, money would rear its ugly head. I was furious with myself for falling deeper and deeper in love with a girl who seemed to be everything I most despised, but I gave in that evening the Redmaynes came to dinner.' He raised her hand and pressed a kiss into her palm. 'You remember that night, don't you, Serena?'

'How could I forget?' she asked softly, touching her lips to his in a kiss that deepened with the sweetness of memory, and went on and on as Leo pulled her gently down with him into the softness of the sofa.

For a while explanations were forgotten and they gave themselves up to the sheer joy of being able to touch each other and hold each other and kiss without restraint, and it was only when Leo tried without success to untie the knots in her apron that the mood was broken and they began to laugh at his frustration. He shifted so that they lay side by side and Serena could disentangle the knots herself.

'It didn't look nearly so difficult when you took it off that night,' he pretended to grumble. 'Why are you always wearing that thing when I want to make love to you?'

'You keep catching me unawares,' said Serena, pulling the ties free at last and tugging the apron over her head. 'See? Easy! All it requires is a little patience!'

'I was the one who was caught unawares,' Leo said, suddenly serious as he rolled her beneath him once more. 'I'd never felt anything like what I felt that night. It was so special that I was sure I must be wrong about you. If I hadn't had to go to that damned meeting I would have asked you to marry me there and then, but I thought I'd wait until we had time together later on when you came into the bank.'

'And when I came in I asked you for money,' said Serena soberly. 'I don't blame you for being suspicious.'

'If only I'd known why! My poor darling, there you were, struggling to support your family and all I could do was shout at you!' He braced his hands on either side of her so that he could look down into her eyes. 'I'm sorry, Serena. You're the bravest and truest person I know. I wish I'd remembered that sooner.'

'It doesn't matter,' she said, pulling him down to kiss her again. 'I wish I'd trusted you enough to tell you the truth, but I was so convinced that I'd never have a future with you anyway. You'd made such a point of saying that you never wanted to commit yourself to anyone.'

'That was before I met you,' said Leo virtuously. 'And how could I tell you that I didn't mean it when *you* were so insistent that you never wanted to get married?' he pointed out with a glimmering smile that widened as Serena blushed.

'Well, I. . .I've changed my mind.'

'Then you will marry me?'

'Yes,' she said, and he kissed her with such tenderness that she felt as if she was dissolving with happiness.

'Look what I brought with me,' he said some moments later, drawing her back to sit next to him as he reached into his inside jacket pocket and drew out the ring she had dropped through the car window. 'I've been carrying this around with me as it was all I had left of you, but now it can go back where it's always belonged.' He slid the ring back on to her finger, and his hands tightened suddenly around hers. 'Are you sure, Serena?' he asked urgently.

'I'm sure,' she said, and kissed him gently. 'I thought I never wanted to get married, but I didn't realise then what it was like to love someone so much you can't face life without them. Being independent doesn't mean anything unless I can be independent with you. Being your wife doesn't mean I'll be any less *me*. I'll be just as I was before. . .but so much happier.'

Leo smiled. 'Does that mean you're planning to carry on cooking for a bunch of overfed bankers who can't tell a pâté from a dog's dinner?' he teased.

'I think Erskine Brookes can carry on without me, don't you?'

'It can,' said Leo. 'I can't!'

Serena smoothed down the lapel of his jacket with a coaxing hand. 'But it *would* be a pity not to use your lovely kitchen,' she went on. 'I've been thinking about producing a range of food for the freezer, and I could do it so much better there than here. . .and it would keep me out of mischief while you're at the bank!'

'As long as you're not too tired for mischief when I come home!'

'Oh, don't worry, I'll still be able to cook a dinner party when you want one,' said Serena innocently, and Leo grinned.

'That wasn't the kind of mischief I had in mind, and you know it!' he exclaimed, pulling her back into his arms.

'Are *you* sure?' she mumbled, emerging from a blissful kiss. 'What about your freedom? Won't I be a terrible tie?'

'I've been free since I left you at the station in Leeds,' said Leo, 'and that's been long enough to teach me that freedom means nothing unless you're there to share it with me. I want to tie you to me so securely that I never have to go through a time like that weekend in Yorkshire again! I was so jealous of Oliver I couldn't think straight.

'That night. . .well, I was determined to keep my pride but when it came to it I couldn't keep my hands off you, and you were so sweet, so loving, that I was going to throw pride to the winds and beg you to stay with me, but when I woke up it was to find that you'd gone off with Oliver.' He took her face in his hands. 'Don't do that to me again, Serena!'

'I won't.' She laid her palm against his cheek, and leant forward to give him her kiss as promise. 'I'll never leave you.'

'And I'll never let you go,' said Leo, holding her close. 'We've wasted enough time as it is.'

She rested her head back against his shoulder and smiled at the reassuring glint of the diamonds on her finger. 'It's wonderful not having to pretend any more!'

'The pretence is over,' Leo agreed. 'Now we can get on with the reality. There's only one thing worrying me. . .'

'What?'

'You hate weddings,' he reminded her and Serena smiled as she kissed him again.

'I've got a feeling that I'm going to change my mind about that too!'

Free Gift Offer

With a Free Gift proof-of-purchase
from any Harlequin® book, you can receive
a beautiful cubic zirconia pendant.

This stunning marquise-shaped stone is a genuine cubic
zirconia—accented by an 18" gold tone necklace.
(Approximate retail value $19.95)

Send for yours today...
compliments of ◈HARLEQUIN®

To receive your free gift, a cubic zirconia pendant, send us one original proof-of-
purchase, photocopies not accepted, from the back of any Harlequin Romance®,
Harlequin Presents®, Harlequin Temptation®, Harlequin Superromance®, Harlequin
Intrigue®, Harlequin American Romance®, or Harlequin Historicals® title available in
February, March or April at your favorite retail outlet, together with the Free Gift
Certificate, plus a check or money order for $1.65 U.S./$2.15 CAN. (do not send cash) to
cover postage and handling, payable to Harlequin Free Gift Offer. We will send you the
specified gift. Allow 6 to 8 weeks for delivery. Offer good until April 30, 1997, or while
quantities last. Offer valid in the U.S. and Canada only.

Free Gift Certificate

Name: _____

Address: _____

City: _____ State/Province: _____ Zip/Postal Code: _____

Mail this certificate, one proof-of-purchase and a check or money order for postage
and handling to: HARLEQUIN FREE GIFT OFFER 1997. In the U.S.: 3010 Walden
Avenue, P.O. Box 9071, Buffalo NY 14269-9057. In Canada: P.O. Box 604, Fort Erie,
Ontario L2Z 5X3.

FREE GIFT OFFER   084-KEZ
ONE PROOF-OF-PURCHASE
To collect your fabulous FREE GIFT, a cubic zirconia pendant, you must include this
original proof-of-purchase for each gift with the properly completed Free Gift Certificate.

084-KEZ

Happy Birthday to

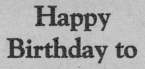

It's party time....
This year is our
40th anniversary!

**Forty years of
bringing you the best
in romance fiction—and
the best just keeps
getting better!**

To celebrate, we're planning
three months of fun, and prizes.

Not to mention, of course,
some fabulous books...

The party starts in **April** with:

Betty Neels
Emma Richmond
Kate Denton
Barbara McMahon

Come join the party!

You're About to Become a *Privileged Woman*

Reap the rewards of fabulous free gifts and benefits with proofs-of-purchase from Harlequin and Silhouette books

Pages & Privileges™

It's our way of thanking you for buying our books at your favorite retail stores.

Pages & Privileges™

PROOF OF PURCHASE HR-PP23

Offer expires March 31, 1997

**Harlequin and Silhouette—
the most privileged readers in the world!**

For more information about Harlequin and Silhouette's PAGES & PRIVILEGES program call the Pages & Privileges Benefits Desk: 1-503-794-2499

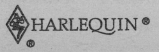

HARLEQUIN ®